Call Me Alli

~

REGINA FELTY

To my daughter, Sara.

You've come so far and your story is not over yet, sweetheart!

Prologue

We all have a story.

Often, we are unaware of what the next chapter holds for us, but life goes on anyway. We can either participate in the crafting of our story or just be surprised by what happens next.

Sometimes, it's both.

Whether we admit it or not, God is the true author of our life's story. He already knows where the story ends, but God rarely indulges us with spoiler alerts that give away his plan. If he did, we wouldn't experience the authenticity of discovering our story as it unfolds: the good and the bad.

But I am also an active part of my story. God isn't just throwing out random experiences to see how I will react, shocking me again and again with unexpected curve balls. Instead, I'm given the honor of writing some of the scenes, selecting parts of the dialogue, and choosing whether I respond with grace or fight the author (God) every step of the way.

It's been a journey, figuring out God's plan for me. Some of the plan—this story of mine—still remains a mystery.

But I have to ask: What kind of story am I leaving behind for others to read?

I won't see the full story unfold and understand why I faced the struggles that I did until the last chapter is written and God puts the final period on the last sentence of my story. I strive to not question the plot twists that constantly uproot my expectations and do my best to trust the process because, well…my story isn't over yet, right?

~

Strength and honor are her clothing.
She shall rejoice in time to come.

Proverbs 31:25

Chapter One

THE BRIGHT LIGHT STABS THROUGH MY CLOSED EYELIDS, and I instantly flinch and grab wildly for a pillow to shove over my face.

"Harper!" I yell.

The light flicks off, and a timid "So sorry" comes from somewhere near the door in the now dark-again room. Instead of reaching for my phone to look at the time and bring on another bout of light blindness, I mumble from under the pillow, "What time is it?"

There's a brief silence before she replies. "2:27."

I drag the pillow from my face but keep my eyes screwed shut. "In the *morning*?" I whine.

"Uh . . . yeah," she says.

The silence is thick, but I know she hasn't moved. "Harper, you can't just stand there in the dark all night." I sigh. "Just turn the light on."

Instead of reaching again for the switch closest to her, I hear her shuffle toward her side of the room. Suddenly, there's a crash, and something falls to the carpet. "Sorry," Harper whimpers. "I knocked a picture off my nightstand."

I roll my eyes, but, of course, she can't see it.

"You don't have to keep apologizing. Just hurry up."

As soon as I say it, there's a muted *click*, and her desk light illuminates the room, the dome shape of her lampshade casting a glow over the lower half of the room.

I instinctively screw my eyes closed but peek one eye open a second later to test my light tolerance. The brightness is more subtle than the overhead room light had been. I open both eyes.

Harper sits on the edge of her bed, both thumbs dancing rapidly on her phone screen. She's fully dressed, although her clothes are a bit rumpled. Her long, brown hair is scooped up into a messy topknot bun. Her jaw dips into a big yawn as she lifts her chin to look at me. Between the lamp and her lit phone screen reflecting off her glasses, I can't see her eyes as much as I can *feel* them looking at me.

"What are you still doing up?" I ask. "Isn't your first class at 8:00, as in five hours from now? And where were you anyway?"

She stifles another yawn. She knows I'm not just being bossy, even if my just-got-rudely-awakened tone is sharper than I intend. Harper and I have this unspoken agreement to help one another stay accountable.

I'm not that great of a student, but I try to stay on top

of my grades and study hard. It's not for lack of trying; it's just that I have to work a lot harder than most other students, especially in math and science.

Harper is super smart, and when she applies herself and stays focused, she breezes through her classes. The problem is, Harper can't stay focused to save her life. She's like a little bird that flitters about, chasing one butterfly to the next. I'm constantly having to throw a net over her to reign her back in. I guess that spontaneity and spunk work well for her as an art major, but her creative energy has a tendency to bubble over at the most inopportune moments.

Harper finds clever and fun ways to help me memorize mundane facts for tests and keeps me entertained when I start to drag in my studies. And I help her keep her feet on the ground by hanging a copy of her upcoming assignments on the wall, then loading her down with guilt when she starts to wander down the path of procrastination and distraction.

It's a symbiotic relationship that works great for both of us.

Harper leans over to pull her tennis shoes off, then tosses them off the end of her bed, which irks me because, after all the times I've tripped over her shoes, books, empty food containers—you name it—I've asked her a thousand times to keep her things picked up. But I'm too tired to bring it up tonight. Correction: I'm too tired to bring it up *this morning*.

"I decided to work downstairs in the study room. I didn't want to wake you," she says.

Hmm, which is exactly what you ended up doing anyway, I think.

It's my turn to yawn. "You were studying all night? I don't remember there being any upcoming tests on your schedule for today. Did you forget to tell me?" I glance over to the assignment paper tacked on the wall above the desk.

Her hands work at freeing her imprisoned hair from the black band wrapped around it. "Not exactly." She grins sheepishly. "I fell asleep."

I roll my eyes again, making sure she sees me do it this time. "Good one, Harper."

"Oh, be quiet, *Mother*," she says. She pulls a floral nightgown out from under her pillow and lays it across her lap before tugging her T-shirt over her head. "If I wanted your opinion, I'd tie a note around a rock and throw it at you." Her chin lifts as she pretends to scan my bed from top to bottom, then tilts her head to investigate under my nightstand. When she's finished, her head nods with satisfaction and she smiles. "Nope, no rocks or notes in sight," she mocks. "Guess I didn't need your opinion after all. Now, go to sleep." Harper throws her shirt at me, and it lands on my face.

I rip it off and throw it right back at her. "For your information, Miss *Harper-Not-My-Mother*, I was asleep before you decided to come tromping in here and light up the room like a Broadway show."

She taps a finger against her cheek and looks thoughtfully at the ceiling. "I think *tromping* is a little exaggerated, don't you think? I believe my entrance was more stealth with a touch of suspense." She shrugs. "Think about it. If I hadn't flipped on the light to show myself, you might've heard me in the dark and thought I was a serial killer instead of just sweet, harmless Harper."

I stare at her in bewilderment. "You are the weirdest person I have ever met, Harper."

She manages to slip her sweats off and wiggle into her nightgown while we talk. Then, she rolls her T-shirt and pants into a ball and tosses them to the floor, the bundle landing directly on top of her tennis shoes. Her brows lift like she's proud of the accurate shot, but then she looks over and notices my face. "Don't worry, I'll pick them up in the morning," she says. Jerking back the covers on her bed, she sinks down on her pillow and tugs the sheet to her neck before leaning over to turn off the light.

I close my eyes and let the darkness settle over me, the heaviness slowly luring me back to my dreamless sleep. My body grows heavy, and my breathing slows as I descend deeper into oblivion. But just before the final twinkle of consciousness fizzles out, Harper's voice breaks through the fog.

"Honestly, Alli, aren't you glad I wasn't a serial killer?"

"Go to sleep, Harper," I growl.

Chapter Two

ALL THE GIRLS HAVE A CRUSH ON PROFESSOR ANZLER, OUR American Literature teacher.

When he walks around the room, which is more like someone taking a stroll through the park with the relaxed and easygoing way he carries himself, you can almost hear the sighs from the females as he brushes by each student, the tips of his fingers resting briefly on a few desks in his passing as he elaborates on literary tropes like irony, metaphors, and hyperbole. Even the way he enunciates *hyperbole*, with the slightest emphasis on the "hy," brings on blushing smiles hidden behind fingers.

It's not that I'm immune to Professor Anzler's charms. His gentle disposition and quiet voice that barely raises above sea level, even when he's lecturing on a passionate topic, leaves you feeling soothed no matter what kind of a day you were having before you walked in his classroom. His salt-and-pepper hair, full mustache, and neatly groomed beard with regal hints of gray melting into dark give him a distinguished appearance.

Professor Anzler's dark brown eyes are deep pools of compassion that have the power to tame even the rowdiest guys in class, who are usually bent on stirring up some kind of excitement when they get bored in class. With broad shoulders and perfect posture, Anzler reigns over his classroom with a majestic air that demands everyone's undivided attention.

During our second class at the beginning of the semester, Professor Anzler casually mentioned that he'd been a men's business attire model in Europe ten years ago. I've never seen phones tugged out of pockets and bags so fast, including mine, as we all hurried to Google old photos of Jared Anzler.

"So, tell me what you're feeling about what you've read so far? What's the setting for Maggie look like right now?" Professor Anzler stands in the middle of the room and swoops in a wide circle, arms open, pulling the whole room into a big, warm hug.

We recently started reading *Maggie: A Girl of the Streets* by Stephen Crane and were told to be ready to discuss chapter one in class this morning. A guy in the front of the room, wearing a navy-blue ski cap pulled low over greasy, brown hair, raises his hand.

"Scott." Professor Anzler points at the ski-cap guy, who

turns around in his seat to face the professor and the rest of the class.

"Yeah, well, I'm already getting the vibe that there's a lot of degradation and some heavy violence going on in Maggie's life. The setting in chapter one is pretty intense and kinda depressing," Scott says. "I mean, it *is* the slums of New York City." He shrugs. "Would you expect anything different?"

Professor Anzler is already nodding. "Good observation, Scott. Intense, right." Then, addressing the entire class, he adds, "Do we agree with Scott? Maggie's situation seems pretty dismal and depressing already, wouldn't you agree? What kind of a mood are you feeling already from this passage—Andrea?" He taps Andrea's desk with one finger and smiles down at her.

She's beaming up at him like she's a puppy he's just adopted and brought home. "Well," she sighs, never taking her eyes off the professor, "I immediately felt depressed by the end of the first chapter. It was, I don't know . . . *dark.*"

Another soft tap on her desk and a smile, and Professor Anzler looks up and says just one word: "Dark." He nods thoughtfully and drops his head, a crease forming between his brows. As if speaking only to himself, he adds, "And we will continue to see this tone, this mood, throughout the story." He shakes his head sadly, as if he's about to walk into a room where he knows something awful waits but can't be avoided.

He lifts his chin and squares his shoulders, visibly shaking off the melancholy. "Let's pause there. I want you to continue reading through chapter three. We'll pick this conversation up again tomorrow."

"Professor Anzler," a timid girl's voice calls from somewhere behind me. "Tomorrow is Friday."

She's right. We won't have class again until Monday.

"Ah, correct." Professor Anzler nods, cupping his chin and rubbing a finger down his lips. "In that case, read on through chapter four."

He moves to the front of the room, shrugs out of his blazer and tosses it on his desk chair, then uncaps a dry erase marker. Before turning to the board, he announces, "I want to go over some key vocabulary for this unit. You might want to copy this information down because there just might be a quiz on these terms in the near future."

We all know what that means: a quiz is *definitely* coming up in the near future. I'm already prepared with a blue spiral notebook and mechanical pencil laid out in front of me.

Zach would be so proud.

I smile when I think about my high school classmate from science who was the most studious and organized guy I've ever known. It was almost annoying at times how nerdy and smart Zach was. He'd rescued me more than once with loaned markers, pencils, and science notes that I'd failed to take myself during class. *He'll probably become a neuroscientist or brain surgeon someday,* I think as I pick up the pencil, flip open the cover on my notebook, and fix my attention on my professor.

Chapter Three

"ALLI, CAN I SEE YOU FOR A MOMENT?"

I zip my bag closed and swing it over my shoulder as I make my way to the front of the class. "Sure, Professor."

Professor Anzler finishes a notation on the board, caps his marker, and sets it down in the tray. "Have a seat."

He motions toward a straight, wooden chair next to his desk before pulling out his own chair. I sit in the chair he indicated and balance my bag on my lap as he lowers his tall frame down until he's eye-level with me. I'm aware that I'm alone with the handsome professor, and, suddenly, my hands feel clammy. A quick glance at the door confirms that it's wide open and that there are students walking by in the hall. I'm not the least bit concerned that Professor Anzler would behave inappropriately toward me, but I've seen how some of these college girls stare at him during class, and I know they'd jump straight to the worst conclusions about him and me if they were to stumble across us with a door closed, no matter how innocent our interaction may be.

Professor Anzler picks up a pencil from his desk and taps it against a stack of papers in front of him. Leaning back in his chair, he tilts his head to the side with a slight nod.

"So, I heard something about you."

My stomach does a quick flip, and my thoughts hit the gas as I try to imagine what he's referring to. *Has someone been talking about me? About what?* I don't take my eyes off him, but my imagination is playing ping-pong off the walls of my head, searching for a place to land.

"Oh, well, I can't imagine what. I lead a fairly boring life," I say, trying to act nonchalant, when I'm really a bundle of nerves.

He chuckles and shakes his head, the pencil going still in his fingers. "Sorry. That sounded cryptic. Shall I try that again?"

My mind says, *Yeah, that would be a great idea*, but my mouth answers, "Maybe."

Maybe? What kind of an answer is that?

My clammy hands have escalated to sticky, and I wipe them on my jean skirt, hoping the professor won't notice. I can't figure out why I feel guilty when there's nothing to feel guilty about. Unless, of course, he produces a sufficient reason why I *am* guilty of some unknown infraction, and the sticky hands are justified, and I should be ashamed of myself for . . . well, whatever it is I did. I know I haven't plagiarized on any of my assignments and—

"I heard from a reliable source that you applied for an internship with *Evangelism Today* recently." A large smile dominates his face, and one salt-colored strand of hair falls against his forehead. My tension starts to dissolve.

The imagination ping-pong rolls to a stop, and I exhale air I hadn't known I was holding. I give a second swipe of my damp palms across my skirt before answering.

"Oh, yes. Yes, I have." *Is that proper English: Yes, I have?* "Um, how did you hear that I'd applied for an internship?" I return his smile, but a new strand of anxiety crawls up my spine.

He waves a hand in the air. "Oh, I happen to have a good friend on staff there. He and I were having lunch last week, and he mentioned that one of the students from this college had applied and thought they were also enrolled in our journalism program. Of course, that piqued my interest, and, well, I may have asked for the student's name." He grins sheepishly.

"Ah . . . I see. I guess it's a small world out there," I say, sinking lower into my seat, not sure where this conversation is leading.

"Yes, you could say that." His brows come together in a worried crease. "I hope you don't mind, you know, me inquiring about the intern position. I guess it's only natural for me to take an interest in my students."

"Oh, no . . . No, it's fine," I rush to reassure him.

"There's nothing secret about it. Applying for an internship with *Evangelism Today* was one of the reasons I'd wanted to attend USC in the first place: so I could be close by. It's not a big deal," I manage to fumble out, even though I think I *do* kind of mind. There's something disarming about knowing that your college professor and prospective boss have been casually discussing your professional life over their lunch hour. Who wouldn't feel weird about that? So, even though I *said* it wasn't a big deal, it *is* kind of a big deal.

But Professor Anzler is already nodding his head, clearly accepting my answer and moving on. "Good, good. It will be a great experience for you."

"Well, if I'm chosen, that is," I hurry to say, not wanting to seem as though I'm assuming acceptance of the position. "It would be a dream come true for me."

The professor stands and pushes his chair in. I quickly stand as he reaches out a hand. His dark eyes are warm and friendly as he grips my hand in a firm handshake.

"I don't see any reason why this dream won't happen for you, Alli."

"Thanks," I say, returning his smile. "I appreciate your confidence in me."

Chapter Four

"I KNOW, MOM. I ALREADY TOOK CARE OF THAT," I SAY, exasperation creeping into my voice. "Aaand, yep, that's already been done too, thank you very much."

Mom's harassing me about my car registration—*again*—which isn't even due for another twelve days, but whatever. Whenever we talk on the phone, Mom always spends the first five minutes of our call going over a list of things she feels she needs to remind me about, even going so far as to ask me what I've eaten for every meal that week.

I shake my head, wondering if she keeps a running list on the refrigerator labeled "Things to Nag Allisandra About." Using my full first name, Allisandra, would be appropriate, too, because that's what she calls me when she's about to have a serious conversation with me. It's her cryptic way of warning me that she's going to be doing most of the talking and that she expects to be listening.

When she calls tonight, after barely asking if I'd had a nice day, she launches into her standard twenty questions, which include inquiries like: have I been getting enough fresh air, am I keeping up with my laundry, and so on, inevitably sneaking in a question about if my roommate, Harper, is inviting guys to our dorm room (she's not). Then, she caps it off by asking me whether I've kept up with my flossing.

I'm not even kidding.

"*Really*, Mom? You know I can't afford floss." I can't resist teasing, although it's not too far from the truth. As a full-time college student, even eating Top Ramen is a luxury some days.

When Mom laughs, I know I've made my point.

"Okay, I'll leave you alone," she says. "How are classes going?"

My eyes drift over the array of books fanned out across my bed and the open notebook nestled on my lap, the pages already full of notes though I'm only half done with homework for the night. I'm currently drowning in research for an objective essay for my American Lit class, and the only thing I've heard in my head all evening is Professor Anzler's voice drilling into us that our facts must be *verifiable, verifiable, verifiable.* I glance over at my desk, where there's another notebook and two novels that I'm supposed to read to compare narrative styles for my English class. I haven't gotten past the cover of either of them.

I don't dare tell my mom that I'm teetering on the edge

of overwhelm, though. I don't need the additional torture of her distress. The more Mom worries, the more questions she asks, which leads to more tension for me. With both of us stressing, it's a recipe for an emotional disaster.

"They're going great," I say.

I'm not lying. *Tonight*, classes are going great. *Tomorrow* . . . when I'm falling behind on assignments and on the verge of tears, they'll be less than great. That's the reality of my life right now.

I shove the notebook off my lap and pull my knees to my chest, settling back against the pillows to give my back a break from several hours' worth of being hunched over. I'm constantly worrying I'll end up a hunchback when it comes time for me to finally walk across the stage to receive my college degree.

"How's Avery?" I ask, steering the conversation onto a safer topic.

There's a soft snort on the other side of the line. "Oh, you know Avery. She's ten going on sixteen. Can you believe she's already asking for a cell phone? She claims that all her friends have one. Dad told her we would talk about it when she's in middle school."

"*Middle school?*" I whine. "Are you serious? That is *so* not fair! You wouldn't let me have a cell phone until I was sixteen, Mom. Why are parents so strict on the firstborn child, only to become weak jellyfish with the next kid? Not cool."

The truth is, Avery isn't really my sibling. She's my

cousin. My Aunt Marg died when Avery was six, and she came to live with us. We've thought of each other as sisters since then. Neither of us had other brothers or sisters, so we instantly connected. We've always fiercely supported each other and argued and fussed like genuine blood siblings. I'd always wanted a younger sister, and Avery needed someone to look up to, especially during that turbulent time of her life.

We needed each other.

"To be honest," Mom continues, "I help out a few days a week at Avery's school, and a lot of the fifth and sixth graders actually do have cell phones now. In fact, I've seen third and fourth graders with them. I think that's pushing it a bit early though."

"Wow." I mutter. "How in the world did I ever survive elementary school without a way to communicate with my parents and friends—and I guarantee it's more about the friends than the parents—without a cell phone?"

Mom and I drift off into our own thoughts for a moment before she says softly, "She misses you, Alli."

Alli, instead of Allisandra. My heart softens.

Her words hang in the air, while thoughts of home and family and the comfort of the familiar poke holes through my attempt to build walls of independence and self-sufficiency.

"I miss her too," I whisper. *I miss you all*, my heart says.

The only other sounds around me are the hum of the small refrigerator sitting on a table in the corner and the grinding and squeaking of a truck passing below the dorm window. You never know what to expect with the comings and goings of a college dorm. It's either as quiet as a monastery while everyone is off to classes or away for the weekend, or it sounds like the end of the day on Wall Street as everyone scampers about to finish trades before the final bell sounds for the day. Well, at least how Wall Street *used* to sound before it modernized.

"Well, anyway," Mom says, shaking out of her reverie. "I'm glad you got your car registration out of the way."

"Yep," I say.

"And have you already made an appointment for your annual physical?"

My mother. She just can't help herself, can she?

"Yes, Mother. I'm not hopeless."

"Uh huh," is her only reply.

Chapter Five

HE HASN'T CALLED OR SENT A TEXT IN THREE DAYS.

I feel the anger stewing to a boil inside me.

It's not like Anthony and I talk every day or anything, but we haven't gone more than two days without talking since I moved to California. It's become a ritual for us—a very cozy one, I must admit—and I hadn't realized how much I'd come to look forward to his calls most nights.

"It's fine. No big deal," I say aloud to absolutely no one as I throw my cell phone in my satchel, yank the dorm room door open, and almost plow into Harper. She stands with a hand outstretched, reaching to open the door, which I've obviously beat her to. She hugs her backpack and a half-empty Starbucks cup in one arm. The hand reaching for the door pulls back to reach for the Starbucks cup instead, which she now holds out to me. "Want some?"

I scrunch my nose and shake my head. "Uh, no.

Thanks anyway." I step back and make room for her to enter. "I'm on my way to a meeting," I say as she scoots past me into the room.

I catch a whiff of caramel from her coffee and whatever concoction of essential oils Harper applied this morning. Harper is all into essential oils, and our dorm room always has a fog of scents hanging in the air from the two diffusers strategically placed in two opposite corners of the room. The scent lingers in her wake. *Ylang Ylang and lavender? And how do I know this?*

Harper dumps her backpack onto her desk and spins around to face me. I'm still standing at the open door with my hand on the knob, watching Harper like a hotel porter waiting for a tip.

"Meeting? What meeting?" she asks, confusion written on her face. It takes Harper a few seconds longer than most to register things.

I glance down at my watch and realize I've got thirty minutes to catch my bus and get across town, and I need to scoot if I'm going to make my meeting by 9:30. "The meeting with the Assistant Editor at *Evangelism Today*. I told you about it last week, *and*"—I point over at the calendar hanging on the wall above my desk— "it's on there, not that you ever remember to look at it," I say with a self-righteous tone.

She's looking at the calendar as if it's the first time she's seen it as I pull the door closed behind me. I can't engage Harper right now or she'll prattle on and never let me out of here. Like I always say, Harper and time have a rocky relationship.

I make it to the bus stop in front of the USC campus on time and settle into a seat next to a sleeping old man whose chin bobs against his chest in cadence with the bumps and potholes the bus bounces over. It was either this seat or the one next to a rough-looking guy with torn jeans and AirPods turned up so loud I can hear his headbanger music from where I sit three seats away. I settle back on the bench and close my eyes briefly, my breathing slowing as the effects of only five hours of sleep last night weigh on me.

The bus rocks gently side to side as we maneuver through busy city traffic. Other than the faint hum of a talk show the bus driver is listening to on the radio and the muted pulsing of AirPod dude's music behind me, the bus is blissfully quiet. If I'm not careful, I'll soon be joining my bench partner for a nap and miss my stop.

I peek over at the old man and wonder with concern if he might have already missed his. Or maybe he has no destination or anything better to do but to ride the bus out of sheer boredom.

I mentally run through my brief phone conversation with the Assistant Editor of *Evangelism Today* magazine—*What was his name again? Oh, right, Isaac Holmes*—and how he told me that they were only considering taking on a handful of college interns and that I would primarily be working on research projects if I'm chosen. A sigh escapes my lips and I roll my gaze over to watch the old man's head press against the bus window. The dingy grime on the glass makes everything on the other side appear grungy and depressing.

I turn away, pulling my phone out of my bag and scrolling through social media for less depressing things to look at. That, and I need a more pleasant distraction to keep me awake.

Research work is *not* my favorite, and it isn't what I was hoping for as my first dip into real journalism, but it would be a gold star on my resume. Experience that would, hopefully, push me forward in my writing career. I imagine myself sitting in the journalist seat, tapping out award-winning articles that are sought after by several top publications while my research assistant gathers all the mundane details that I'll no longer have to spend my time finding.

I smile to myself and shake my head. *Keep dreaming, Alli. Research is part of your life for a long time, whether you like it or not.*

But this research-only internship is only temporary. I can do this. Of course, I haven't even had my meeting with Isaac Holmes yet, and I'm only assuming I'll be accepted.

What I really need to do is find a real job. Real in that it would provide a steady paycheck. At least a little extra something. I wouldn't need, or have time for, a lot of work hours because I'm already bogged down with coursework, but a few hours a week would be a start. I got a few decent scholarships, and Mom and Dad are paying for most of my college expenses, but I still need cash for all the extras that come along with being on my own.

The bus wheezes to a stop, and I lean forward to peek

out the window again to see where we've stopped. My stop is next.

I rest my shoulders back into my seat and jerk my head toward my seat partner, who now snores softly against his chest. *Do I wake him? What if it's not his stop, and I disturb him for no reason?*

I'm agonizing over deciding about the old man, one that I'd better hurry up and make before the next stop, when a woman enters and makes her way to a seat behind me. Before the doors close, I reach over and gently tap the old man on the shoulder.

"Excuse me. Sir?"

He jumps, and so do I.

"I'm so sorry," I say, stricken that even my soft tap nearly caused him a heart attack. "I . . . I mean, is this your stop by any chance?"

The old man coughs loudly and pushes himself up with arthritic hands, blinking rapidly and looking like he's forgotten where he is and wondering why this woman sitting next to him is rudely interrupting his nap.

He blinks a few more times, glances out the window, and shakes his head. "No," he says in a raspy voice. "Blankenship Road."

It's a good thing we weren't at the Blankenship stop because the bus is already moving on.

"Oh, um, so sorry," I stammer.

The old man looks over at me, smiles, and inclines his head before reaching into his jacket pocket and pulling out a small paperback. He rests the book on his lap and, with gnarled and shaky fingers, presses it open to a page that has been earmarked. Then, he lifts the book to within a few inches from his face and starts to read, softly mumbling the words under his breath.

A faint buzzing sound comes from the seat between us, and I realize it's my cell phone. I'd stuffed it back into my bag. Shoving my hand into the front pocket, I pull out the vibrating phone and see that it's Anthony.

My heart jumps with a sudden thrill. *I need to find a cool ring tone for him one of these days,* I think, and hurry to tap the accept button and press the phone to my ear.

"Hello?" I whisper, turning my body away from the old man for privacy. Then, I turn and see the dude with the AirPods staring at me. I spin back around.

"Alli?" His voice is soft and crosses the hundreds of miles between us so effortlessly that it feels like he's sitting right next to me. For a moment, I forget that I'm angry with him.

"Yeah, it's me."

"Did I wake you? Is this a bad time?" he asks, which prompts me to glance at my watch and see that it's now 9:14 and I've got sixteen minutes to make it to my meeting. I look up and notice my stop up ahead and press the phone between my ear and shoulder while I scoop up my bag off the bench and push myself to the edge of my seat.

"No, not at all." I think of the time again. *When was the last time I slept in until after 9:00 in the morning?* I wonder. I also think about how I told him last week about my meeting with Isaac Holmes from *Evangelism Today*. Disappointment settles in my chest as I wonder how he could have forgotten something so important to me.

Three days of not calling. Forgetting something that was a big deal to me. *What's going on with him—with us?*

"I'm actually on my way—" I debate reminding him since it obviously wasn't as important to him as it is to me. I'd hoped he would have called last night, or at least this morning, to wish me good luck. But . . . he didn't.

The bus hisses to a stop, and the doors open. I bounce down the three stairs, and my feet are barely on the curb before the doors *whoosh* closed and the bus pulls away.

"Wait. What did you say?" he asks. "Sorry, I couldn't hear you. What's all the noise in the background?"

I make my way over to press the button to cross the street and start scanning signs on buildings across the street, looking for *Evangelism Today's* signage. I spot the sign two doors down from the Wells Fargo on the corner. "I said I'm on my way to a meeting," I say loudly into the phone since there's now a crowd waiting to cross. "I'll call you later, okay?"

"Oh, got it," he says. "Oh, wait, is this that meeting—"

"Gotta go, Anthony," I pause only a second and think I hear him mumble something on his end. But I don't wait. I end the call and jog across the street. I don't stop until I'm inside the building and waiting for the elevator doors to open. Checking my watch again, I see that I have seven minutes to get to the fourth floor.

"Great first impression, Alli. Barely making it on time, much less *early*," I scold myself. I had hoped to slip into the restroom to tidy up and still have time to spare. Now, I'll show up flustered and out of sorts instead of put together like I had hoped. I pull out my phone and tap on the camera icon so I can check my smile for telltale signs of breakfast. I run my tongue over my teeth and feel the grime. *Oh, gross, I forgot to brush my teeth this morning. Could this day get any worse?*

Thanks a lot, Anthony.

I know I'm being unreasonable, but I'm desperate to transfer the guilt somewhere other than on myself.

Chapter Six

I give my name to a refined older lady with overly bright pink cheeks and a toothy smile and tell her that I have an appointment to meet with Isaac Holmes.

"Please have a seat, Ms. Mancini, and I'll let him know you're here," she says, pointing one glossy, red fingernail toward a huddle of wooden chairs in the corner of the room.

I nod and make my way over. I perch myself on the edge of a chair, ready to spring up the moment Mr. Holmes makes an entrance. I nestle my bag against me on my lap and take in my surroundings.

"Ms. Mancini," I mumble to myself. The designation feels way too formal for me and hangs like an oversized coat on my tongue. *I hope they don't plan to call me Ms. Mancini when I work here. I'm not that old yet. Well . . . if I work here.*

My fingers dance nervously on my knees as I scan the

room. A tall plant with glossy leaves in a ceramic pot sits next to my chair. I can't resist reaching out to pinch one of the leaves to see if it's real. The edge crushes in my fingers, and I jerk my hand back. *Yep. It's real.*

Under my feet, a series of multicolored, geometric patterns march across the large area rug. The pattern makes me dizzy, and I shake my head and look toward the large bookcase on the opposite wall instead. I notice several Christian fiction books that I recognize and a whole shelf of nonfiction books that I don't. Naturally, there are several issues of *Evangelism Today* magazines displayed prominently on stands on the top shelf.

Seeing the magazines sends a sense of dread through me. I try to swallow, but my mouth is so dry that my tongue sticks to the roof of my mouth.

Why hadn't I remembered to read the last few issues of the magazine? I could've at least been up to date with a few of the current articles. What if Mr. Holmes asks questions about what I thought about the articles? What would I say? "Oh, I really don't know about that, Mr. Holmes. I haven't even looked at your magazine since the January edition." Good job, Alli.

"Ms. Mancini?"

Despite my intention to be relaxed and ready to meet with Mr. Holmes, on hearing my name, I snap to attention, causing my bag to slide off my lap and onto the floor. "Yeah? I mean, yes, that's me," I say, my words tumbling over themselves like rocks bouncing down a hill.

Naturally, I *had* done some spying on the magazine's

website and on social media, checking out who Isaac Holmes was and seeing if I could get an idea of what kind of person to expect when I met him. *I should have spent that time learning more about* Evangelism Today *instead of its Assistant Editor*, I think, regret snaking through my chest. Isaac Holmes is taller than he looks on social media, and the sharp angles of his face seem much less imposing in photos than they do in person. His dark brown hair compliments his hazel eyes, but the hints of curved lines around his mouth look more like frown lines than smile wrinkles.

I tamp down my racing thoughts and reach for my bag, one hand slipping down to grab my bag off the floor as I keep my eyes on Mr. Holmes, who smiles stiffly and makes no move to lend a hand.

My fingers wiggle into empty air, searching desperately for the handle of my bag.

Finally, I break eye contact to look down, snatch the handle, and stand, thrusting my hand out. "And you must be Mr. Holmes."

His handshake is firm and brief. "Good to meet you, Ms. Mancini. Right this way."

He turns and starts walking back to an office behind the pink-cheeked secretary's desk, and I trail behind, feeling like I'm on my way to a doctor's exam room instead of an interview. The secretary gives me a little wink as I pass her desk, and I feel some of the tension ease. Secretaries that wink at you must be a good omen, right?

Mr. Holmes' office is spacious and formal, the focal point of the room being his oversized, dark wood desk and a black leather desk chair. Two matching leather armchairs face the desk, and Mr. Holmes motions to them.

"Please, have a seat."

As he makes his way around the desk to his chair, I study the large floor-length window behind his desk and imagine myself taking up residence in an office like this. First off, I'd ditch the prudish wood desk for a white one with a gold stapler and a vase of fresh flowers. Of course, with that window view overlooking the city and the botanical garden located on the grounds—which is where I would sit to read on the bench next to the climbing roses— I'd probably spend more time daydreaming than working.

"So, Ms. Mancini. Why don't you tell me a little about yourself and why you are interested in an internship with *Evangelism Today*."

I blink, the bench and climbing roses fizzing out of my vision. I focus my attention back on Mr. Holmes.

He smiles warmly, but his hands are clasped formally on his desk, and his posture is tall and straight.

I wiggle and straighten in my chair.

"Oh, of course. Yes. Well . . ." *Get it together, Alli. You and Harper practiced these questions over and over.* "I'm a freshman at USC, and I'm majoring in Journalism. In high school, I was on the yearbook staff and wrote articles for our school newspaper. Writing has always been a passion—"

"Yes, I see that," Mr. Holmes interjects, glancing down at an open file on his desk. *Where did he pull that out from? That file wasn't there a minute ago.* He lifts the top page of what I now recognize as my resume with some hand-scribbled notes written on it and sets it to the side.

I squint, trying to read the writing, but it's too small, and I'm not even remotely skilled at reading cursive upside down.

"What about now?" he continues. "What kind of writing do you do now, or what publications have you been involved with at USC?"

I swallow the ball of spit in my mouth and pray I don't start coughing as it sticks in my throat. "I, um, I haven't really checked into a lot of . . . that." *That? I'm majoring in English and Journalism, and I can't express myself with words better than* that? "I was going to get settled and get a feel for campus life first," I continue, "then look into applying for some of the campus publications near the end of next semester." I trail off, feeling like I'm digging myself into a deeper hole rather than making things better.

"Oh, which publications at USC were you considering?"

I was being truthful. But honestly, I'd only skimmed the student publications and hadn't put any serious thought into where I wanted to focus my efforts.

Noticing that I'm slouching again, I square my shoulders and attempt to appear confident. "Well, I was thinking about the *Daily Trojan.*" Then, deciding I need to make my case stronger, I add, "*SCene Magazine*, another of USC's student publications, was on my radar too."

He's nodding, but I can't tell if it's a sounds-like-she's-on-the-right-track nod or a she-hasn't-got-a-clue gesture.

This guy is impossible to read.

"Yes, *SCene Magazine* would be a good start," he says.

One foot taps against my chair leg with nervous energy and I have to cross it behind my other leg to steady it.

"You understand that we have some strict requirements for an internship here at *Evangelism Today*," he says. "Do you think this would be good for you to pursue right now if you are . . ." He glances down at my resume as if searching for his next words on the page. "still adjusting to college life and your course load?"

My hands grow clammy as I realize the fatal mistake I've made in using the excuse of adjusting to college as my reason for not researching campus publications.

He's right. I'm not ready for this internship at all. I might as well just march myself out of this office right now. Stupid. Stupid. Stupid.

"Yes, sir," I say, trying desperately to backpedal out of this. "It's not that I'm overwhelmed or don't have time for work outside of my courses. It's just that this internship was —*is*—my focus and priority. I didn't want to commit to other publications if I was accepted for this internship. I would want to give my full attention to *Evangelism Today* instead of dividing my time between an internship and other projects."

I'm not sure where that answer spawned from, but I'm

sure glad it did because it's a pretty clever one. It's not a lie either. If I get this internship, I wouldn't want to be tied up somewhere else as well. Even though the internship would mostly involve boring research while other publications would allow me to do actual writing assignments, working for this magazine would open doors that are more suited for me, especially as a Christian. I'd had a lot of fun writing about high school interest topics and interviewing athletes and club members for articles, but college publications would be on a whole new level for me. I might be required to take on writing assignments that conflict with my faith or just don't hold much interest for me. So, I'd always wanted to get my foot in the door of a faith-based publication that would align with my beliefs and would be about things I enjoyed writing about. Even doing research work as an intern would be a step in the right direction and at least give me an opportunity to learn something about behind the scenes of the magazine industry.

So, why don't you just be honest and tell him all of that?

Mr. Holmes scribbles something at the bottom of my resume, but, again, I have no clue what he's writing. He sets the pen down, folds his hands over the page, and fixes his smile back in place. "I see. That does make sense, and I can appreciate that you would be focused on your work here rather than trying to juggle your schoolwork with other commitments." Lifting his hands, he closes the top of the file folder that holds my paperwork and sets it to the side.

"So, I understand that one of your professors at USC is Jared Anzler. Am I correct?"

I'm sure the color has drained from my face. *Why is he bringing up Professor Anzler?*

"Uh, yes, that's right. Professor Anzler teaches my American Literature class."

"Hmm, of course," he says, and this time his smile seems genuine. "He and I are colleagues and good friends. We go back a long way." He doesn't elaborate or mention anything about his lunch conversation with the professor. He has to know that I'm curious about how he knew that Jared Anzler is my college professor.

It's on the tip of my tongue to ask Mr. Holmes what his point is in bringing Professor Anzler up, but I can't find a way to phrase it that won't sound awkward.

The opportunity slips away as he pushes his chair back and stands. His warm smile from moments ago has wilted and the formal expression is back in place. "Well, Ms. Mancini, we will be in touch, hopefully in the next week or so," he says as he walks me to the door.

I turn and shake his hand once again, disappointment churning in my chest. He barely asked me any questions and didn't go into any further details about the internship opportunity, so I have to assume he's politely dismissing me. I can't deny that my feelings are a bit crushed.

"Thank you, Mr. Holmes," I respond, pasting on a smile I don't feel. "I really appreciate you meeting with me today, and I look forward to hearing back from you soon."

The smile disappears as soon as I turn away and know he can't see my face. My confidence is shattered, and I'm sure I can smell the smoke of my dreams going up in flames.

I walk past the secretary, not daring to even look her way. If I do, I'll burst into tears.

Chapter Seven

I'm in the middle of an epic yawn when I hear my name. My eyes feel like someone stuffed cotton balls in them as I look up and see Professor Cromwell, my Studying Narrative instructor, staring at me. "Well," she says, eyebrows raised. "A double shot of espresso might help with that." I see humor dancing in her eyes behind her thick black frames, but I'm still mortified that I'd nodded off during her class. Mercifully, she turns to the board and starts writing.

"So, as I mentioned, you will have two options," she says. "One, you may write a true story based off your own experience but writing it as if it were fictional. That includes using fictional characters and writing in third person. Or, two, you could choose to write a completely fictional story, telling it in first person. Writing in first person will make your story feel closer to a personal narrative." As she talks, she makes two columns, writing the descriptions for each choice under their proper heading. Her short, gray hair swishes back and forth as she moves across the board.

Then, she finishes and caps her marker before setting it on the tray and turning back to the class. "The choice is yours. Be creative, and remember to incorporate a lot of dialogue to draw the reader into your story. I'll be looking for the components of a story arc with . . ." She turns back to the board and uncaps her marker again, starting a bullet list on the board. She looks over her shoulder, marker poised in air. "Who can tell me what a story arc includes?"

I'm quick to raise my hand in hopes of redeeming myself. "Background information. An introduction," I say.

Professor Cromwell nods, now facing the board. "And what is that called?" she prompts.

"Exposition?" I answer. I'm almost certain I'm using the correct term, but my brain is still in a fog, and I'm not positive that I trust my answer.

"Correct. Exposition." She writes the word, and I breathe a sigh of relief.

Another student at the back of the room chimes in: "Conflict. Rising action."

The professor is ahead and has already added the words to her list. "Yes. Then, there's our all-important climax, then falling action, and, finally, the anticipated resolution. However!" She spins around, fingers still gripping the marker as she uses it to punctuate the air. "The writer can choose to throw in an unexpected resolution or one that the reader has been hoping for all along. That's the thrill of being the author of the story! These"—she points the marker over her shoulder toward the list on the board behind her—" are all parts we should easily identify in your story, but there should be a whole lot going on in the process. It's the process that I want you to impress us—your readers—with." She gestures to the board again. "Decide which journey you will take us on and have fun!"

She beams and caps her marker with a flourish. Several students giggle at her enthusiastic antics before opening their laptops and getting started.

I've already decided that I want to write my story from a fictional approach but based off a personal experience; I'm no good at writing in first person narrative. But I can't decide on what experience I want to write about.

I could write about my disastrous meeting with Isaac Holmes yesterday. Just the thought of looking like a fool in front of him and the certainty that he would no more consider me for an internship than he would cosign a loan for me makes me wish I could just go back to the blissful unawareness of sleep once more.

With my thoughts in a jumble and my stomach in knots, I watch Professor Cromwell as if inspiration might drift over to me from her. She sits on a high stool, balancing her laptop on her lap even though there's a podium three feet away, as if the effort to walk over there would disrupt whatever groove she's in and isn't worth it. She taps away at something on her keyboard, her long fingers graceful as they glide across the keys.

Professor Cromwell is one of those human beings who seems to have it all together. She's obviously well-educated, runs marathons and has the slim, tan body to prove it, dresses like she's twenty-five instead of closer to sixty, and is a published author. Sure, everyone starts somewhere, and she had to put in her time writing essays and stories like the rest of us, but there's just something about her that makes me feel like she probably breezed through that as well. Even the photos of her and her family on her desk look like they could have been clipped out of magazines.

I did overhear a few students one day in study hall mention that her husband passed away a few years ago and that they'd seen her flirt with the IT guy. It does seem like he's always dropping by to fix something on the interactive whiteboard or reconnect her printer. If it's true, I think the IT guy is way below Professor Cromwell's station and, honestly, too young for her. But it's none of my business. She looks up suddenly and catches me staring at her.

Great. That's twice that she's caught me spacing out instead of working.

She closes her laptop and stands up.

Oh, no! Please don't come over here!

I lean over and snatch my laptop out of my backpack, jerk up the lid, and start tapping on keys. The problem is that my laptop hasn't even finished waking up yet. Anyone sitting behind me and paying attention would notice that, and I'd look like an idiot.

I don't have time to worry about that, though, because Professor Cromwell has made her way over and is staring down at me. I pause a moment to give the impression that I hadn't noticed her yet.

"Alli. Do you need any help getting started on your story? Have you decided what kind of story you want to write?"

I've managed to type in my password and bring up a blank Google Doc. At least I look legit now if she peeks over. "Oh." I look up at her with what I hope mimics surprise. "Yes, I plan to write a fictional piece using a personal story, but I haven't decided where I want to go with it yet."

She taps one manicured fingernail on the edge of the table, a thoughtful expression on her face. "Well, are there any memorable events in your life that made an impression on you? Something exciting or life changing? Or, if you're comfortable with it, you can revisit a painful or traumatic experience."

I blink up at her. *Revisiting a painful experience is the last thing I want to do*, I think.

"Often, the hardest part of writing, as you know, is just getting started," she continues. "That first sentence, the first paragraph. It might help to jot down several ideas first and see which of them inspires you. Some writers are successful diving right in, others work better with an outline."

I already know all this but nod like I don't. I know I won't be able to feel inspired right now. My inspiration for writing tends to hit late at night and when I'm alone. However, I've been trying to conjure up inspiration for this story—late at night included—for a few days now and still haven't got a clue what I'm going to write about. More than likely, based off past experience, I'll come up with some last-minute idea and whip out a story in one night. I guess I just work better under pressure.

"Thanks, professor. I'll put some more thought into it." I'm hoping she'll move on and leave me to wallow in my uninspired state of mind.

"Well, let me know if you need any help," she says and moves to chat with the girl next to me.

I stare at the blinking cursor on my still-blank screen and try writing that first sentence, just to test her theory of "just getting started."

Tulane stared out over the crowd, every eye riveted on her, the people hanging on her every word like their next breath depended on it. They adored her, wanted to be like her. If they only knew the truth. That Tulane was not who they thought she was. If they knew, they would cast her out, perhaps even stone her. She couldn't—wouldn't— let that happen. The only person who knew the truth about her was Ravon. He alone had the power to destroy everything she'd built. With Ravon destroyed, her secret would be safe.

I look over the words I've just vomited on the screen. *Nine sentences. Not bad! But where in the world did that opening paragraph come from?*

I sense movement around me and look up to see others around me packing up to leave. I snap the laptop closed and push it down into my backpack, assured the file will be saved in Google Drive.

I'm still not sure what to make of what I've written, but at least it's a start.

Chapter Eight

"So, have you had any run-ins with a crocodile yet?" I ask.

"No, no crocodiles. But I see alligators all the time. There are even parks where you can pay to go see them, but I wouldn't bother," Brynne says. "You don't have to go far to find alligators. My grandpa sees them all the time on the golf course."

Brynne and I had become good friends the last half of my senior year of high school. We'd been classmates for a while but hadn't really hung out together. She ended up coming to church with me and became a Christian. Our friendship deepened after that, and, although no one could ever replace Tessa as my best friend, Brynne had come pretty close. While I'd decided to attend college in California, Brynne had gone to live with her grandparents in

Florida so she could attend the University of South Florida to pursue a pharmacy degree.

"Alligators . . . crocodiles; I don't care which. I have no interest in ever meeting either one face-to-face," I say. "So, how's school going?"

"Well, good thing is, you're in no danger of seeing either one where you are. You keep your earthquakes; I'll live with the swamps and alligators," she chuckles. "As far as school, I'm not exaggerating when I say that I feel perpetually exhausted and am drowning in an ocean of homework. But I love every minute of it."

I roll my eyes. "Of course you love it, Ms. West Morrison High Valedictorian. Hours of homework and piles of paperwork are what you live for. Classrooms are your happy place."

"Oh, stop being so dramatic, Alli. I do have a life outside of school," she says.

"Really? Like, what do you do for fun these days, Brynne? Decorate your bedroom with pages torn out of textbooks and listen to educational podcasts on rerun?"

"Ha ha. Very funny," Brynne says. "For your information, I've joined the girls' volleyball team at church and go bowling twice a month. Oh, and I'm also learning to knit. How's that for a brainiac? Besides, what do *you* do for fun since, apparently, hitting the books is beneath you?"

"Oh, sure," I huff with mock annoyance. "Having fun isn't even on my radar. Who has time for fun? Some of us have to work a whole lot harder than others to earn passing grades in our classes. But I have to say, I'm impressed with the knitting pursuit. Who's teaching you to knit?"

"There's a girl in my microbiology study group that always brings her knitting projects to work on while we wait for the rest of the group," she says. "I asked her one night to teach me, and we hang out for a while after study group to knit. We've actually become good friends too. In fact, she's coming to church with me this Sunday."

"Wow, Brynne! That's awesome that you've made new friends and are inviting them to church. I've met a lot of great people in the youth group here, but I don't really hang out with them much outside of church stuff. Like I said, I don't have time."

"You have to *make* time, Alli. You were the one who first invited me to go to church with you, and look what great friends we became after that. Homework and endless papers and quizzes aren't going anywhere for the next four years. Some people won't always be around. You have to invest in *people*, Alli, not isolate yourself behind academics." She laughs. "That's some profound advice coming from a scholar such as myself."

"I know, Brynne. You're right. I guess I just don't feel up to investing in new friendships. It's exhausting," I say, trying to put humor behind my words but still feeling like they ring true anyway. "I just don't feel like I need more than you, Tessa, Kristin, Anthony, and some of my other friends in Tucson. Why invest in long-term relationships when I won't see most of these people in a few years? Everything I need is back home in Arizona."

"Are you listening to yourself?" Brynne says, sounding like a mother scolding a toddler. "A few *years*? Seriously, Alli, you can't put your life on hold for a few *years*! And, in case you haven't remembered, I'm in Florida, not Arizona, my dear. And Tessa won't sit around forever, waiting for her long-lost best friend to make her way home from college. She needs to make other friends and to get out of the house and hang out with new people."

Why does Brynne have to be so logical? And so . . . right?

I hadn't really thought about why I hold myself back from forming meaningful friendships with any of the girls at church. Maybe I just don't feel like I fit in with them. It's not their fault I feel that way either. Everyone in the youth group has been super cool and always includes me in stuff. Am I just making excuses because I'm afraid of getting hurt or used again? Am I letting the painful experiences I had in Tucson with Tessa and the kids at school overshadow me here? Tessa and I have moved past all that. In fact, we're closer than ever. So, why don't I even try?

"Point taken," I say. "You're right. I'll try harder."

"That's the spirit, Alli. Go make friends. Leave your mark on those folks in California. Before you know it, we'll all be back together again with degrees on the wall and the future wide open to us. Who knows? Maybe you and Anthony will be planning a wedding by that time. At least I *hope* so after four years," she mutters. "I'll still have some college ahead of me, but we have to make a promise that none of us will run off and make a life in another state without the others following."

"Oh, sure, Brynne! Like it could be that easy," I say, my words dripping with sarcasm. Let's just make it through this school year before we start talking about matrimony and where we're going to settle in four years, okay? That's all I can handle thinking about for right now."

"Fine," Brynne says. "But I better be one of the brides-maids in your wedding."

Chapter Nine

"You know this book is two weeks overdue, right?" The guy behind the counter asks.

I smile shyly at the girl standing next to me in line and shrug before turning back to the guy, staring at me with an annoying smirk on his face.

USC has an ample selection of good fiction in its many libraries, but, today, I decided to come to the public library because I get tired of hanging out on the college campus all the time. I needed a change in scenery outside of either amped-up-on-caffeine or half-dead-from-staying-up-too-late college students. On top of that, there's a cozy coffee shop a few doors down that makes the best white chocolate mocha lattes in town. I guess this is what I get for changing things up.

"Uh, yeah, I guess so," I mumble. "Do I owe money or anything? You know, for being late and all?"

He shakes his head, but the smirk remains. "Nah, I can waive it. Not sure the two bucks would be worth—" He turns the paperback book over and reads the title again. "*Redwall.* By, uh, Brian Jacques." His eyebrows raise as he looks up at me. "Isn't that a story about talking animals?" His lips twitch with humor.

I give him a patronizing smile, ready to be done with this humiliating moment and Mr. Smirk. The girl next to me waits patiently and appears to be more amused than irritated.

"We're studying anthropomorphism in my English class. You know, it's—"

"Animals with human characteristics," Mr. Smirk finishes and pushes the book off to the side. "I get it." He turns his eyes to me and his smirk morphs into a warm smile, all traces of teasing fading from his face. "I was just messing with you, though. I actually love the Redwall series. I collected all the paperbacks when I was in middle school and just handed them down to my little brother a few years ago."

Since I don't really know how to reply to this, I just nod. He continues to stare at me, like he's waiting for me to confess my mutual adoration for the woodland creatures of Mossflower Woods, who do, indeed, have conversations with one another and live in harmony at the cozy Redwall Abbey. As a matter of fact, I did get pulled into the story of the heroic Martin the Mouse and all, but I wouldn't admit that to this guy in a million years.

"Um, yeah, I guess it was a cute story. I couldn't totally see how a kid could be into the books," I say, nonchalantly. "But I'm more into dystopian novels."

His smiles widens. "Oh, like *Lord of the Flies* by William Golding?" he asks, his eyes brightening like there's no doubt I'll agree with him.

I shake my head. "No, I'm more of a *Hunger Games* kind of girl."

While he makes an entry on the computer, which I assume is the adjustment to my late fee, I study Mr. Smirk—now Mr. Friendly and Sincere. I take notice of the light-blue T-shirt he's wearing that's imprinted with *I tried being normal once. Worst two minutes of my life.* It seems out of place for a library clerk, but, hey, what do I know about library clerk etiquette? His curly, black hair falls to his shoulders, and a galaxy of freckles splash across his face and tumble down his neck. His light-green eyes and fair skin conflict with his long, dark curls, giving the impression of an Irish poet wearing a pirate wig.

A loud sigh from the girl tells me that her interest in our conversation has waned and that it's time for me to move along. I agree and slide my bag from the counter and slip it over my shoulder.

I cough out a fake chuckle and take a step back from the counter, making room for the impatient girl to fill the space. "Well, thanks again for, uh, waiving that late fee." I take another careful step back, as if I'm afraid that moving too quickly might make him change his mind about the fee or launch him into another book discussion.

"Don't let it happen again, Allisandra," he says with a wink and reaches for the book the girl hands him.

I stop and stare at him, but his attention is already on the other girl, and he's dismissed me.

Allisandra? How does he know my real name? Everyone here only knows me as Alli.

I slowly turn and make my way to the exit. Passing between the sensor bars and through the automatic glass doors of the library, I'm still racking my brain for clues on how the guy had known my real name. I already know my library card has Alli Mancini printed on it, so that can't be it. I mean, Harper knowns my name is Allisandra, but even she doesn't call me that. Besides, Harper has never been to this library with me—I can't see Harper in *any* library—so that possibility would been out.

It's not until I'm behind the theater building back at the college—my new favorite place to be alone—sitting on a bench under a large tree with its dense canopy blocking all but a few persistent rays of sunlight, that I register Library Guy's final wink when he said my name. My *full* first name, which still freaks me out. I mean, I don't think twice when a cute, old man winks. In fact, I find it quite charming. But the guy at the library, that I have a gut feeling is close to my age, winking and teasing me makes me feel weird.

Was he flirting with me?

I know I've never been the sharpest at deciphering a

guy's intentions toward me, but I've learned a lot from Anthony these past few months of dating-not-dating. That's what we call it: *dating-not-dating*.

It's more of a joke between us because I told Anthony before I went off to college that I wasn't ready to date him —that I was still trying to just figure out my life first. Yet, I'd agreed to him calling regularly so we could test out how compatible we were, and now the lines between dating-not-dating have become almost nonexistent. Since he calls several times a week and I look forward to and, honestly, have come to depend on hearing his voice and seeing him on screen when we FaceTime, I think it's obvious that we're more than compatible. And I'm pretty sure Anthony feels the same way about how the relationship is going. In fact, on screen, there've been a few times Anthony has winked at me playfully, and it never fails to stir up the kaleidoscope of butterflies that seem to have taken up residence in my stomach.

I have to admit, Mr. Library Guy is kinda cute, but I didn't notice any butterflies or even one flutter when he winked at me. I take that as a healthy sign that my feelings for Anthony are legit.

I take a bite of the protein bar I've dug out of my bag and feel an unexpected smile tug at my lips as I wonder what Anthony would think if I told him some guy at the library was flirting with me. Would he be jealous? Would I *want* him to be? I guess I'm flattered that Mr. Library Guy noticed me, and I find myself reaching up to touch my hair and wonder what it was that he found appealing, *if* he found me appealing.

I've always seemed to be noticed as being *different*—which didn't always equate to a positive thing—especially with how I look and dress as a Christian girl. In the high school scene, where girls often feel the need to look just right, to have the perfect makeup and hair, designer clothes, and flawless skin—the whole package—my modesty and *plainness* (that label always hurt the most) made me feel as if I stood out like an unsightly weed in a garden of roses.

"Ugh, stop it, Alli. Why are you thinking about this?" I say aloud, then do a quick scan to make sure no one overheard me talking to myself.

I know why my thoughts have wandered here. I've grown up a lot lately, but sometimes I still feel the sting of growing pains.

Finding out who the real Alli is hasn't been easy. In fact, I'm still figuring out her true identity. She's like an ornery fairy darting in and out of the shadows, daring me to catch her. Some days I almost do. The figuring-out-Alli part of me doesn't ache like a broken tooth anymore. It did not too long ago—through most of my high school years, in fact. But all that is behind me now.

At least I hope it is.

Being proud of who I am and accepting my *different-ness* has brought me a lot of peace, and I feel like I'm finally becoming comfortable in my skin. My faith feels just a little stronger now, and how I present myself as a woman of

God, inside and out, is something I've chosen to embrace and am learning to love. Growing up, I think I'd blindly followed my parents' faith and just went along with what I'd known and been born into. But on my own now, away from home and my family, I'm free to make my own choices. I never felt that my parents or anyone else forced me to live a certain way or shoved Christianity down my throat, but now I've faced the crossroads myself and chosen my own path.

An elderly couple makes their way up the path from behind the theater building, and it strikes me as odd to see them walking on a college campus where they're obviously way past the age of the normal passerby. My eyes drift over the nearby landscape, and I take in the lush, low-hanging branches of the trees, the well-manicured grass, and the large terra-cotta pots overflowing with seasonal flowers and bright-green ferns. Then, I look back at the couple. They must live close to the college and are out for a stroll on the grounds. I would probably enjoy a leisure walk through here too. I guess I just haven't found the time to fully enjoy my surroundings here at USC.

Maybe when I'm old, I think, *I'll have time to walk arm-and-arm with my best friend and life partner as we just enjoy each other's company.*

The couple never looks my way as they move past me, quietly mumbling sweet nothings to each other—her face aglow with a smile that transforms her wrinkled face, revealing a glimpse into a more youthful past. The elderly gentleman with her walks straight-backed and has the woman's arm tucked firmly into his as he walks beside her. Her frame is bent and frail, and her feet shuffle as she ambles alongside the man. I can tell he's slowed his pace for her and is careful to guide her over any uneven spots on the path that might trip her up.

I smile to myself as they pass on the other side of a group of trees and move out of sight. It's like they'd unknowingly sprinkled happy dust over me as they passed. Seeing life as it could be in my future, with a doting spouse and time for strolls through nature together, fills my heart with hope for the future.

There's so much more to life than I can imagine.

Chapter Ten

"OVER HERE, ALLI!" A TALL GIRL WITH BRONZE SKIN AND shoulder-length braids waves both hands in the air to get my attention.

Balancing my paper plate so my hot dog doesn't roll off the side, I make my way over to the far corner of the room where several young adults are crowded around a circular table. The tall girl beckons me over and points down at a folding chair next to her.

I offer the group my best smile. "Hey, guys," I say as I set my plate down and pull the chair closer to the table.

Several faces look my way and smile back.

"What's up, Alli?" This comes from a guy across from me who has braces and bright-auburn hair, the same color as my mom's hair.

I knew his name last week when I met him after the Sunday morning service, but I can't for the life of me remember it now. I'm the worst when it comes to names. "Hey!" I nod and offer a little wave.

The girl who'd motioned me over is Kris. I remember her name because I repeated it to myself a hundred times while driving home from my first service at Grace Center Church.

"Hi, Kris. Thanks for the seat."

She gives me a playful nudge with her elbow. "Well, we aren't gonna let you sit all by yourself and eat, right?"

Everyone turns their attention to a guy on the other side of the table, who's talking about a great deal he got for a bass guitar he found on eBay. When he starts going on about frets and scales and other guitar jargon that I know nothing about, I start to lose interest. But I nod and try to act like I'm following just to be polite and because I'm the new girl in the group and don't want to act like I don't care, when, in reality, I don't care one bit.

I'm relieved when Kris leans close and asks, "You have anything going on Saturday night?"

I turn toward her in, hoping my enthusiasm with the distraction from guitar talk isn't too obvious, and shake my head. "No. Why?"

"A few of us were thinking of going ice skating and just hanging out. Wanna come?"

A quick glance around the faces at the table reveals that most of the females have also checked out of the guitar conversation. A few have pulled out cell phones to browse through, while some just sit with bored expressions on their faces.

I turn back to Kris. "Yeah, sure. That would be fun! I don't really know how to ice skate, but I guess I have to learn sometime, right?"

We both laugh, and she picks up her phone from the table. "Give me your number, and I'll text you with the details."

We exchange numbers and spend the next few minutes chatting about where we grew up and about our families.

When I tell her that I grew up in Tucson, Arizona, her eyes widen. "Aren't there a bunch of tarantulas and hyenas there?"

I laugh. "Well, we do have tarantulas, but I've never seen a hyena. However, javelinas are native to Tucson."

She giggles. "Oops, that's what I meant: *javelinas*."

I scroll through my photos until I find what I'm looking for, then hold it up for her to see. "My mom saw these two when she went on a walk early one morning." The photo is of two javelinas that had been roaming near our neighborhood, digging through a bag of trash someone had left on their driveway.

Kris takes the phone and stares at the photo. "Eww, they look freaky," she says, handing the phone back to me. "Are they dangerous?"

I take the phone and slip it into my pocket. "They can be. Mostly they're just a nuisance. Especially around Halloween when some of the neighbors put jack-o'-lanterns on their porches. The javelinas tear them up and leave a mess."

"No way! I wouldn't want to find one of those things on my porch. I'd go after it with a shovel."

Chuckling, I reply, "Actually, my dad runs outside with an airhorn and scares them off. It's hilarious to watch them stampede down the road."

Kris looks horrified.

Some of the guys are getting up from the table, and I hear one mention that they're going to go in the church and jam on the instruments for a while. None of the girls are interested, so we end up staying at the table and talking along with the rest of the guys.

Suddenly, I find myself the center of attention as all eyes turn to me.

"So," a guy with sandy hair and ruddy skin calls to me from across the table. "Did your whole family move here?"

I shake my head. "No. I moved here for college. I'm actually living on campus at USC."

A brunette next to me pipes in. "I'm a student at USC too," she says. "I live at home with my parents, though. I think it would be cool to live on campus."

There are five of us at the table, and we talk about college for a while before moving on to books we're reading, our families, and other casual conversation.

During a brief lull in the conversation, the guy with braces throws out, "Do you have a boyfriend?"

Everyone turns their attention back on me again, eyes lit with interest.

I just nod. There's no need to explain that Anthony and I are still maneuvering our way through the unknown territory of a long-distance relationship.

My eyes dart around the table. Four heads lean forward, expecting me to spill the details.

"Um, his name is Anthony."

Kris makes a low *aww* sound next to me and asks, "How long have you guys been together?"

I think about her question. *Together* suggests that Anthony and I came to an understanding around some specific time frame and have been an item since then. I don't want to be evasive, but I don't know how to explain to this group that I don't even know when he and I became a *we* or where *we* are headed as far as our relationship goes.

I want to crawl under the table, but hiding isn't an option, unfortunately.

"Well, we've been talking for several months now, but it's not serious or anything—I mean, not yet. It's kinda complicated. We hadn't really become official before I moved here, and sometimes, I'm still not sure—"

"Long distance relationship," the brunette says. "I get it."

"Yeah, you're so right, Chloe," Kris says. At least I know the brunette's name now: Chloe.

Several heads nod in agreement. Chloe shoots me a sad look. "So, it's you who's holding the relationship back?"

Am I? I know Chloe means no offense with her question, but it stings anyway. *Is Anthony still holding out hope that we'll take our relationship to another level?* I think about the conversation we had before I left for California, when he told me how he felt about me and asked if he could date me.

I told him no.

It's not the answer he wanted to hear and definitely not the one that I wanted to give him, but I was struggling with a lot of confusion about where my life was taking me. In fact, I still am. I didn't think it was fair to encourage the spark we had just to struggle to keep it alive while we lived in two different places. He accepted my answer with grace and maturity, not that I would ever expect anything less from Anthony, who's as honorable and mature as any guy I've ever met. I conceded to cultivate our friendship by talking on the phone once or twice a week so we could see how things went. And . . . that's how it's been going so far.

I sense that the girls are waiting for my answer. I lift my shoulders and let them sink with a deep sigh. "Yeah, I guess so."

Chloe pats my arm with maternal tenderness. "We'll be praying for you, Alli, that God will show you what he wants for you and Anthony."

A few other girls chime in with an "Amen," and Kris gives me a playful punch on the shoulder—much different from Chloe's gentle pat. "We've got ya, girl."

I feel like I've just gotten pulled into a big group hug. It feels kinda nice.

Chapter Eleven

"HOW DID YOUR MEETING WITH THAT MAGAZINE GO?" Harper asks.

"By *that magazine*, you mean *Evangelism Today*?" I give her a pointed look. I guess I should give her credit that she even remembered. It's better than Anthony had done.

"*Evangelism Today* magazine. Of course, Silly." She rolls her eyes and turns back to the mirror to finish braiding her hair. A fog of mist floats around her from a nearby diffuser. The scent is spicy and earthy, and I can't decide if I like it or not. Harper usually goes for the stronger oil fragrances when she's stressed out or trying to hype herself up for a big project.

I shrug, even though she can't see it. "I think it went well." It's not a straight-up lie. I mean, it probably went well in *his* opinion anyway, having eliminated one of the internship candidates so easily.

"His name is Isaac Holmes, the guy I met with. He's the Assistant Editor."

"Okay . . ." Harper says, still with her back to me. "So, what does 'went well' mean? Did you get the internship or not?" Her tone is clipped and agitated. I don't take it personally since her essential oil choices have already clued me in to her frame of mind.

I'm working to refill my mechanical pencil with lead when a piece of lead breaks off in my fingers and lands on the floor under my chair. I lean over to look for it, but it's impossible to find on the dark shag of the carpet. "I don't know yet." I groan and slip off the chair to my knees to get a closer look. "He said I'd be hearing something back from him soon." *Like a confirmation that I didn't make the cut.* I spy the broken lead piece under the table leg and stretch my arm out to reach it. Pinching it between two fingers, I come up under the table and bang my head. "Ouch!"

Harper spins around, a bottle of body spray in her hand. "What are you doing down there?"

"Praying," I growl, rubbing the sore spot on my scalp.

Harper huffs and turns to shove the spray into a bin on the counter, where she keeps extra toiletries. "Yeah," she snorts. "You need to. Pray for *me* while you're down there. I have a calculus exam this morning."

Well, there's the source of her stress.

"Did you study for it?" I can't help asking, knowing that she probably only crammed for it last night.

"Yes, *Mother*, I did." She huffs again and reaches for a hair scrunchie from the bin.

Pushing myself back up into my chair, I pretend to pray aloud: "Lord, I'm asking you to be with Harper this morning. Let her fail this calculus test in order that she might learn compassion for her roommate and how to have a better attitude."

Harper screeches and runs over to shove her hair scrunchie over my mouth. "Alli! That's so wrong!"

We laugh, and I pull back on the scrunchie and let it fling off my fingers and soar across the room.

Harpers walks over to retrieve it from behind a floor lamp. "No, seriously," she growls. "You know math isn't my best subject, and I'm freaking out about this test." She slips on her sandals and grabs her bag. She's about to leave when I point to her bed. "You left your cell phone."

She groans and races over to grab it and run back to the door. "Gotta go!"

"Praying for you, Harper—for real! You got this!"

I look down at the mechanical pencil, but the lead has disappeared from my fingers again. "Oh, forget it." I fling the pencil onto the table and walk over to look in the mirror.

Frowning at the dark circles under my eyes, I pray they weren't that noticeable when I was sitting across from Isaac Holmes. *Evangelism Today* is looking for chipper, energetic interns for the job—not tired, half-dazed zombies. I turn the faucet to the coldest setting and splash water on my face. *Anthony's going to wonder if he could do better when he sees me on screen tonight.*

Anthony's planning to FaceTime me later this evening. At least that's what his text *said* would happen. We'll see if he comes through.

We've both been running on different calendars and have had a hard time trying to pin down times to talk, although I think he's the one with less time for me than I have for him. I try not to let that worry burrow in too deep. I knew this long-distance deal wouldn't be the best idea for us. But Anthony seems to think the arrangement is just fine.

The problem is, I don't. I hate talking to a six-inch image on a screen and trying to make the conversation meaningful. It feels plastic. It's more than that, too. I miss the smell of his cologne and just being near him. Not that I've told Anthony any of that. It doesn't feel like our relationship is at the level where we share mushy stuff like that.

I grab the towel from the hook to dry my face. It's damp. *Yuck!* Harper must've used it before she left. Another one of those gross pet peeves I have about roommates.

Harper isn't cringe or anything, even if she does have a bad habit of leaving her clothes and books all over the room. At least she's got good hygiene and keeps her clothes and bedsheets clean. Not that those things should matter that much to me. It's not like I'm wearing her clothes and sleeping in her bed.

Throwing the towel into our shared laundry bin, I grab a new one from a basket nearby and hang it on the hook.

Glancing at the clock, I see that I have two hours before my Studying Narrative class. I really should be reading and taking notes right now, but I'd rather go shopping. I can't remember the last time I went shopping for anything that wasn't food or school related. I don't mind going shopping alone either. I'm not like other girls, who won't leave the house without a sidekick tagging along. The downside is that I don't really have any money to spend.

"Oh, well, I'll go anyway," I announce to my image in the mirror. "It'll give me something to do until I talk to Anthony tonight. *If* he remembers to call, that is."

Chapter Twelve

My knees are shaking so bad that I can barely keep upright on my skates, and I haven't even ventured more than three feet from the wall.

Chloe glides up to check on me. "Ok, girl. Had enough practice? Are you ready to take a lap with me and Kris?"

I shoot her a dirty look that is clearly meant to convey: "If you so much as come near me, I'll be flat on my face on this ice."

She obviously doesn't read my look that way because, before I know it, she's motioning for Kris to come over. They position themselves on either side of me and wrap each of my arms up in theirs.

"Alright, let's do this!" Kris shouts above the music blaring and the sounds of squeals and laughter from skaters racing past us.

Grace Center's youth group rented out the whole ice

rink for the night and had more than filled it with as big as the youth group is. Many of them had also brought along guests and family members. The place is packed. I thought it was super cool how we're able to DJ our own Christian music while we hang out with our youth group.

My legs feel like Jell-O, and I sway like a drunken sailor as Chloe and Kris practically drag me between them on the ice. I'm in full panic mode as other skaters sweep past and weave around us. Some of the kids flying by appear to be less than ten years old. I'm mortified. Here I am, almost nineteen years old, and I've never learned to ice skate.

"Come on," Chloe prods. "Move those legs! I feel like I'm dragging around a concrete statue here."

Kris barks out a laugh in my right ear and says, "No kidding. Talk about dead weight. You gotta put some effort into this, Alli, or we're gonna leave you out here to fend for yourself."

I didn't think I could feel more humiliated, but I do. I push my left foot forward and try to push off with my right, attempting to mimic what other skaters were doing, but I only manage to hit Kris' skate and almost send her flying.

"That's it!" I snap. "Abort mission. Take me back to the wall so I can try to recover some of my dignity."

The chorus of "Ah, come on, you've got this" from both girls does nothing to thwart my determination to be back on safe ground instead of in the middle of the Indy 500 of skaters with sharp blades on their feet that I'm sure will end up in my forehead when I go flying over my own feet. Kris and Chloe are huffing from exertion by the time they maneuver me over to the carpeted snack bar area, where they dump me on a bench.

Kris starts to mention that the rink has these trainer walkers made from PVC pipe with wheels on them that I can practice with. "Well, at least I *think* they do," she says. "I know they have them at roller rinks, but I'm not sure about ice rinks."

She moves to look for them, but I grab her arm. "No way. Not in a million years am I rolling around on that ice holding on to a walker."

Chloe laughs. "Seriously, Kris, I wouldn't be caught dead using one of those things either."

Kris shrugs and nods. "Yeah, you're right." She looks down at me and puts her hands on her hips. "So, you're just gonna sit here the rest of the night and watch us skate?"

I fold my arms over my chest with a firm nod. "Yes, I am, thank you. In fact, watching you two will be pretty entertaining. Besides, now that I'm closer to the snack bar, I'll treat myself to a soft pretzel. I need the carbs after all that physical exertion."

Chloe shakes her head, her long ponytail swinging behind her. "You're hopeless." Looking at Kris she nods toward the ice. "Race you." Kris leans over and tugs the top of her sock up. "You're on."

With one last sympathetic glance back at me, the girls take off for the ice. I bend over to unlace my skates.

Tugging them off and casting them to the side, I stand, thankful to feel solid ground beneath my feet again.

I wonder if this is how sailors feel stepping onto land again after a long voyage at sea.

I pad over to the snack bar counter in my socks and order a hot chocolate and a soft pretzel. "Can I get a side of nacho cheese too?" I ask, not caring about all the extra calories I'm about to consume since I probably burned hundreds trying not to nosedive onto the ice.

While I wait for my order, I smile over at the guy next to me, who's also waiting for his food order.

He juts his chin my way. "Whatsup?"

I shrug. "Not much."

The guy is super tall, with a head of loose, black curls that cascade over to one side. I try to remember if I've seen him at any of the youth meetings, but I don't recognize him. Not that I'm surprised. There's a ton of youth at Grace Center. I haven't even met half of them yet.

The older woman behind the counter hands the guy his order, and he turns away without so much as a second glance my way. I don't think anything of it. I mean, I *am* standing here in my socks, and—God forbid—he most likely saw me flailing my way across the rink with Chloe and Kris dragging me. I wouldn't want to be seen talking to the star of the freak show either.

Settling myself back on the bench, I sip my hot chocolate and nibble on my pretzel while I watch the skaters glide across the ice. Like the guy at the snack bar counter, there are a lot of faces I can't place. I've only been attending Grace Center for a short time and have only hung out with a handful of the youth group. And when I say "hang out," I really mean mostly only at church events. I don't get together with any of the youth outside of church stuff, mainly because I don't have the time with trying to keep up with my college coursework.

It's not that I don't want to hang out with them; they seem like a really cool group, and the few I've been around seem pretty sincere about their faith. It's just that with any extra time I have in the evenings, I prefer to spend it chatting with Brynne, Tessa, and Anthony. Well . . . and my mom. When she isn't nagging me, we have some nice chats.

But watching the guys racing around the rink, knocking each other off balance on purpose and sending each other sprawling on the ice, and seeing the girls laughing and teasing each other like they didn't have a care in the world, I can't help but feel disconnected.

Am I lonely? The thought comes out of nowhere and takes me by surprise. *I have plenty of people to connect with from back home. I don't need new friends here.*

At the same time, it hits me that, although I have no shortage of someone to talk to in the evenings, there's still an empty feeling that always hovers after we hang up. Harper makes me laugh, and we get along great, but we don't really hang out. She has her own group of friends, and I, well, I guess I just hang out in the dorm room most of the time.

The thought depresses me.

Wow. I'm turning into a hermit.

When was the last time—or have I ever?—went out somewhere with anyone from here? Tonight is the first time I've ventured away from the norm and actually done something with other youth that wasn't in a church building.

The irony of me watching the youth skating on the rink while I sit alone on a bench isn't lost on me. I finally do something outside of my comfort zone, and I still end up being alone.

I think about how Anthony, Brynne, and I would have Bible studies at the bookstore or how all the youth would go out to eat after youth service. I reminisce about how Tessa and I spent most every night at either one of our houses or went shopping at second-hand stores and yard sales on the weekends.

In Tucson, I was always off doing stuff, but I remember complaining often about not having enough time in the evenings to finish my homework or to work on a writing project for the school newspaper. Now, I have a whole night ahead of me to do just that: homework and writing. But now that the tables have flipped, I don't feel any better. I miss my friends. I miss being with Anthony—actually sitting on the same couch with him, hiking the local trails, or sharing nachos at the park on Saturday afternoons.

And you used to complain about being stuck in Tucson with all the problems you thought you had.

Sure, there was Shanice and Kim, who had it out for

me and ridiculed me for being a Christian. And, of course, there was Chad Barton, who went along with an elaborate prank to lure the good girl—*me*—into believing a popular guy—*him*—was all into her when all he and his friends really wanted was a good laugh at her expense. None of that hurt me as badly as my childhood best friend, Tessa, dumping me to hang out with her new cheerleader friends.

Wow. It's no wonder I wanted to move far away from all that when the opportunity was presented. So why am I so homesick now?

It didn't take me long to arrive at an answer: home is where your heart is. (Cliché, I know.) It's the place where you first set down roots and create lifelong memories. It's where your people are. The place you know best and that feels like a second skin. Even with all its ugliness and potential to hurt you more than anywhere else could, home will always be your Northern star. And no matter how far I go from home, it always seems to be calling me back.

Lord, is this what you meant when you talked about being content in whatever situation we're in?

I pull my phone out of my pocket and search for the scripture. Philippians, chapter four, pops up, and I click the link, reading the words of verse eleven: "Not that I speak in respect of want: for I have learned, in whatsoever state I am, therewith to be content." My eyes scroll down to verse thirteen: "I can do all things through Christ which strengthens me."

Now I'm confused. Was I wrong for not being content back home in Tucson, or am I wrong for not being content here in California? I can't deny that I've done a lot of maturing since moving here and that the change of scenery has been good for me. USC has a great journalism program, and the church I'm attending is an awesome church, with an amazing youth group, even if I do feel somewhat lost in the crowd sometimes. Even then, I know I'd feel more like I fit in if I allowed myself to get involved in some of the other group activities.

"Hey, Alli! What are you doing over here all alone?" My head jerks up to look at the tall woman standing in front of me, her wide, blue eyes sparkling as she takes me in.

How long has she been standing there? "Hey, Sister Reece," I say, greeting the youth pastor's wife with a smile. "Let's just say I'm safer keeping my feet on non-slippery surfaces."

She laughs and plops down on the bench beside me, pulling her long, golden braid forward into her lap. I think I remember someone saying that she's in her mid-thirties, but she doesn't look a day over twenty-eight. With two kids under five years old, her busy life supporting her husband's ministry with the youth, being involved in several church committees, and running her home bakery, I wonder how she keeps it all together physically, spiritually, and mentally. She's thin and dresses stylishly, and she's so cheerful and energetic. Whenever I see her at church, she's always making people laugh or has an arm around one of our girls, praying with them.

I even asked Chloe one time about her, who said, "Yeah, I've never seen her go off on anyone or have anything bad to say about people. Sister Reece is the real deal."

I'm kind of in awe sitting here next to her. I can't remember ever seeing her without a crowd of people around her, and, although she always takes the time to say hello to me, I've never had a full conversation with her. I glance around, half expecting one of her kids to run over or someone from church to show up and pull her attention away. But there's no one in sight besides a few teenagers bantering with each other at the soda dispensers and a guy sitting at a table texting on his phone.

"So, how are you liking things at Grace Center? Are you making some new friends in the youth group?" she asks, turning herself toward me and giving me her full attention. Her eyes soften as she looks at me, and I have this weird feeling that those eyes can see right into my soul.

The thought makes me squirm, and I turn my attention to my pretzel, dipping a chunk of it in the now-cold cheese, then abandoning it in the sticky yellow gel.

"Oh, everyone's been great and has really made me feel welcome," I finally say. "I've been hanging around mostly with Chloe and Kris." I lift my chin toward the direction of the crowded rink as if Chloe and Kris are just passing by in that moment, which they aren't.

She follows my eyes and nods. "I noticed that. They're both great girls. I've known them since they were in middle school and completely boy crazy. Their parents had their hands full back then, but don't tell them I said that," she says with a mischievous wink. "And your classes are going well?"

Her question takes me back for a moment as I wonder how she knows I'm taking college classes, but then I realize that of course she would make it a point to learn about everyone in the youth group. That's just her way.

I turn to set the pretzel plate on the table behind us, all interest in the food gone. "Yeah, my classes aren't too bad this semester."

We're silent for a moment, although the thoughts spinning circles in my head are anything but quiet. I'm still awestruck by the idea that no one else is encroaching on my time with this much-in-demand youth pastor's wife, and I rack my brain for what to talk about while I still have her undivided attention.

"And how are *you* doing, Alli?"

Okay, I wasn't ready for *that* question.

I turn to look at her, trying to judge by her expression if her question was just conversational or leading somewhere else. She smiles and reaches over to pat my hand.

Oh, boy.

"Oh, good—good!" I add with a tad bit too much enthusiasm. "Like I said, classes are pretty chill this semester. No complaints."

"Well, that's wonderful," she says, but the way she says *wonderful* sounds weighed down with suspicion. "Is everything okay with your family?"

A chill creeps up my spine at the ominous question. *Did*

God give her some premonition or something about my family? Did my mom call her? I make up my mind then and there to call my mom as soon as I get back to the dorm later.

"Uh . . . yeah, I'm pretty sure. I mean, last I checked they were all doing okay."

She laughs and gives my hand another quick pat. "Relax, Alli. I'm not trying to freak you out. I'm just checking on you. I know it can be lonely to be so far away from home and from your friends and family. I just want to make sure you're doing alright."

My pulse slows, and I nod. "Thanks. Yes, everything is fine. Honest. I do miss everyone back in Tucson, but coming here was a new start for me. Sure, I wanted to attend USC, but I also wanted to break free from some ugly situations that had been hanging over me for a while. I guess I'm still trying to uncover who the real Alli is and thought that a new place and new faces would help me do that."

She cocks her head, a thoughtful expression on her face. "And how is that working for you? Are you finding the real Alli here in California?"

I shake my head and look back out at the activity on the ice. "Not yet. I'm going to need a little more time to work on that." I look over at her and smile, trying to keep the topic light.

Her voice is soft and maternal as she leans over to wrap an arm around me. "I'm praying for you, Alli. Any time you need to talk or want to pray together, I'm here. Okay?"

My eyes start to sting, and I turn away to blink several times to keep them from filling. I don't dare look at her, because I know I'll end up losing the fight with my emotions.

"Thank you, Sister Reece. You don't know how much that means."

She gives my shoulder a squeeze. "I think I do, Alli."

Chapter Thirteen

I didn't get the internship with *Evangelism Today*.

When I see Isaac Holmes' name pop up on my phone screen, I'm in the middle of a small group discussion in English. Seeing who the call's from, I lose all focus on whatever we were talking about. So do the three other students I'm sitting with. I'm sure the look on my face made them wonder if there was a family emergency or something.

The guy I'm sitting next to nudges my elbow and gets my attention. "You should go in the hall and answer that."

Slipping out the back door of the classroom, I barely manage to tap on the screen and put the phone to my ear just as my phone shuffles Isaac Holmes to voicemail. I let it go and wait to listen, afraid of what I'll hear.

Mr. Holmes is brief and to the point: He's very sorry to inform me that I did not get the internship, that I was so close, but they decided to go with another student, and that if they have another spot open up, I'll be first on the list, *blah, blah blah.* I don't hear much of what he said after that.

Of course, I'm not that surprised; I knew I hadn't made a great impression on Mr. Holmes, so I wasn't expecting to hear, "You're in!" but there was still the smallest sliver of hope that a miracle would come through for me.

Why not me? I think, standing in the hall outside of English class, shaking my head, biting my lip, and trying oh-so-hard not to bawl my eyes out.

The only reason I go back into class after that is because my backpack's still in there. I have to suffer through the "Is everything okay?" and the "What happened?" questions the remaining twenty minutes of the class. Luckily, as soon as class ends, I manage to make a beeline for the back exit door and race back to my dorm room before anyone can ask me anything else.

So here I sit, feeling like a complete loser, shoving the last stale donut into my mouth from the box Harper left out on the table last night. I mean, without that internship, what's the point in being here? I could have attended a college closer to home. Sure, there might be less opportunities for furthering my writing career back home, but if I'm not learning the ropes and getting to practice here anyway, why not make things easier on all of us and go home?

I reel myself back in before my thoughts ramble too far down that rabbit trail. Moving to California wasn't just about the internship but more about starting over and gaining a fresh start in so many ways beyond writing career opportunities.

The donut feels like crumbly paste in my mouth, and I toss the rest in the trash. Noticing a half bottle of water sitting nearby that I'm ninety-nine percent positive is mine, I grab it, unscrew the lid, and chug it down.

Everything has been new and exciting here—just as I'd hoped it would be. But I miss home too. Most of the drama I'd faced and the people who'd given me grief that made me want to flee to California were left behind after high school graduation. But I'm making new friends at the church here and have managed to avoid drama so far, so that should give me peace of mind, right?

I think about my mom and the conversation we had before I made the decision to come to California. She warned me that running from my problems—her words, not mine—wouldn't solve anything and that trouble could find me anywhere I went. She said there was no guarantee that everything would be smooth sailing in a new place. But being a Christian and standing out in high school had been hard for me. I hated the attention, which was usually less-than-affirming and more along the lines of target-on-my-back kind of attention. If nothing else, I know I've done some growing up in the short time I've been away from home. And finding my identity as a Christian has given me a whole new perspective.

I stare at the remaining donut crumbs on the napkin in front of me.

Huh, great new perspective, Alli. One failed part of your plan and you're tucking your tail between your legs and trying to numb the sting of rejection with a stale donut. If you were going to drown your sorrows in a river of sugar, The Cheesecake Factory would've been a way better choice.

A sudden desire to call Anthony comes over me, and I reach for my phone.

I'm about to hit the call button but stop myself. I think about how I've talked for weeks about this internship and how it will be a launching pad to a future career for me. My confidence in being chosen soared high as I filled Anthony's ears with how I'd be the hardest-working intern *Evangelism Today* has ever had and how they'd be offering me a full-time job before I'm even in my sophomore year of college (never mind how I would manage a full-time job *and* keep up with my coursework). Even though he was super supportive and my number one fan, I'm sure it required a lot of restraint for Anthony not to roll his eyes and keep a supportive expression on FaceTime while I prattled on and on. So where am I supposed to find the courage to call him and tell him, "Oh, hey, all that boasting and strutting I did about my shoe-in-the-door intern position? Yeah, well, they rejected me."

Nope.

I set the phone back on the table and snatch the napkin up, not caring that some of the crumbs land on the carpet. I'm not ready to be humbled in front of Anthony yet. It's bad enough that my classmates knew something terrible happened with the phone call in class, and I'm not ready to break down twice in one day.

I hurry to brush my teeth and decide to read the assigned book chapters for tonight in bed. If Harper comes in, I'll pretend I fell asleep reading, so she doesn't try to talk to me. So lame; I know. I just don't feel like talking to anyone right now.

Chapter Fourteen

"Ms. Mancini?"

Of course, I know it's Isaac Holmes. I'd saved his number as a contact on my phone, though I've considered deleting it since I hadn't made the cut for an intern position. What I don't know is why he's calling now, which makes my heart thump with anticipation. *Good* anticipation.

"Yes. Oh, hello, Mr. Holmes. How are you?"

"Doing great. Thanks for asking," he says. I detect a cheerful tone behind his words. My heart thumps harder. "I wanted to let you know that we've changed our minds about the internship position," he says. "With reconsideration, we'd like to offer it to you. Are you still interested?"

Are you serious? Yes! A thousand times YES! I shout at the top of my lungs, but, thankfully, actually only in my head. What comes out of my mouth is much more controlled and refined: "That's wonderful, Mr. Holmes! Yes, I would love to have this opportunity."

"Perfect. I'll have my secretary set up an appointment with you to go over the details and have you sign some paperwork."

He says some other things, but for the life of me, I have no clue what they are. My brain only registers the words *reconsideration . . . changed our minds . . . are you still interested?*

Sometime after that, I know we exchange goodbyes and hear that I should expect a call from Mr. Holmes' secretary. I hope I replied with something intelligent before the call ended.

This time I do shout at the top of my lungs. "Yes!" A less-than-dignified happy dance in the dorm room is followed by a text to Anthony, who's working right now and can't answer his phone; a call to Tessa, who doesn't answer so I leave a voicemail; and a text to Brynne, who's in class right now. I call my mom and dad next. I would have called them first, but I knew it wouldn't be a quick call.

"Guess what?" I say the moment Dad answers his cell phone.

"Internship?" He says, knowing it's the biggest news that would prompt a call from me.

"Wait," I say, not wanting to leave Mom out. "Where's Mom?"

"Hang on a second," he says. "She's in the laundry room." I hear him walking across the wood floor in the hall.

"Trisha!" he calls out. "Trisha, it's Alli. No, no . . . she's fine. Just come over here for a minute."

Of course, Mom would expect the worst first.

When I know they're both listening, I fill them in on the news. I don't have a lot of information for them yet, but I can update them later. Naturally, Mom asks twenty questions, some related to the internship, a few extra thrown in about if I've been eating well and if I'm not staying up too late to study.

"Yes, Mother, I eat and I sleep." I sigh. "I'll let you know more about the internship when I have all the information."

"Congratulations, Alli," Dad says.

"Yes, sweetheart," Mom echoes. "We're so proud of you, honey! How exciting!"

By the time we hang up, I've gotten texts back from Tessa and Brynne but not from Anthony yet. I smile down at the "Way to go!" and the "I knew you had this, girl!" and smile contently. Things just got a whole lot better for me here in California.

"Thank you, Lord," I whisper. "And thank you, Mr. Isaac Holmes. I won't disappoint you."

Chapter Fifteen

I'M ONE OF THE LAST STUDENTS TO LEAVE CLASS, BY MY design. I stop in front of Professor Anzler as he locks the door behind us. I match his step as he makes his way down the hall, and we weave in and out of the incoming traffic of students. "Professor, I wanted to let you know that I ended up getting that internship. You know, the one at *Evangelism Today?*" I don't know why I feel the need to share my news with him. I guess it's because he encouraged me after hearing I'd applied, and now I feel he should also share in my success.

Professor Anzler doesn't break his stride, which I'm actually having a hard time keeping up with since his long legs take two steps for every one of mine. He looks down at me and gives me a beaming smile. "It couldn't have gone to a better candidate, Alli. I'm very happy for you."

My turn to go down the stairs to the first floor is

approaching, so I quicken my steps. Again, I'm not sure why he needs to know what I'm about to say, but I want to tell him the last detail so the story is complete. "Thank you. To be honest, they turned me down at first but then ended up calling me later and offering me the internship. It was a bit of a roller coaster ride for me, but I'm super happy it ended up the way it did."

Noticing I'm slowing as I near the stairwell, Professor Anzler slows his pace to match mine. "I know. I couldn't let them pass up such an excellent opportunity. I might have made a phone call or two to remind them of that." He winks and steps back into the current of students before I have a chance to digest what he's said.

I might have made a phone call or two?

My heart sinks to the floor as I stare at the place where Professor Anzler disappeared and took part of me with him. *No. No. No. He didn't. He wouldn't.* But my head already knows what my heart is trying to reject with all its might.

I didn't get the internship because they wanted me. I only got it because my professor called in a favor.

I feel the jostling of bodies as students push past me, but I don't make any attempt to move out of their way. In fact, I would love nothing more than for someone to pick me up and throw me headlong down the stairs so I won't feel the pain I'm feeling inside right now. I'd been riding on the clouds, thinking that I was special—chosen—a valuable future member of a team, and now . . . now I'm sinking in a deep pit with the sides closing in on me. I want to run, scream, and beat my head against a rock.

How could I have been so gullible? They rejected you once. Didn't you stop and wonder for a minute why they'd changed their minds suddenly?

I'm still standing like a statue at the top of the stairwell when I realize how quiet the hall has become. There are two girls talking at the end of the hall, and a guy dashes into a classroom before the door closes behind him. I'm supposed to be on my way to English class, but there's no way. I'm not going.

It suddenly occurs to me that Professor Anzler could come back this way and catch me standing here. He would surely wonder why I'm still here.

I turn and race down the stairs and across an open grassy area that's a favorite spot for students to sit and relax. But I take no notice of anyone or anything as I make a straight path for my dorm room. It crosses my mind that Harper will be in class right now, and I find relief in knowing that I won't have to worry about answering the questions I know she'd ask the minute she noticed my shell-shocked face.

Two girls walk out of the double doors when I arrive at the building, and the timing is perfect as I brush past them before the doors close. I'm running out of steam, and my thighs burn as I push myself up the stairs in a final burst of energy. When I reach our room, I fumble in my bag for the key, sweat and tears stinging my eyes. I'm barely in the door when I slam it behind me, drop my bag on the table, and throw myself down on my bed, finally able to let loose the flood of emotions that have been threatening to overrun their banks before I could be away from curious onlookers.

I bawl my eyes out into my pillow for fifteen minutes before the tidal wave of emotions settles to calmer waters. I roll over on my back, feeling completely drained.

"I don't need *Evangelism Today* magazine! And I don't need *you*, Jared Anzler!" I scream at the ceiling, as if Isaac Holmes and Jared Anzler are in the room with me. I don't care if anyone else in the building hears me either.

I swipe my sleeve across my snotty nose, not caring how nasty it is. "I wouldn't take your stupid internship now, even if you handed it to me on a silver platter and begged me to accept it," I say, lowering my voice a notch.

I push myself to a sitting position, fury filling my chest with every breath. "I don't need your charity, *Professor Anzler*."

The anger abates, replaced by mortification when I think about how I've told my family, Brynne, Tessa, and Anthony the great news—well, it *was* great when I thought it was legit—and how I'll have to tell them the truth.

Do I really have to tell them the whole truth? I think.

Part of me is beyond grateful that I hadn't had the chance to tell everyone that the magazine rejected me first before calling me back to retract their words and offer me the internship. Of course, now I know the reason for the abrupt change in the decision.

No, I'll just tell everyone that Mr. Holmes called back and apologized, saying that he'd been mistaken, and they couldn't offer it to me after all.

Of course, that's a lie.

As far as *Evangelism Today* is concerned, they think I'm going to be interning with them. They don't know about the conversation with Professor Anzler and how I'd rather die than be offered the job just because my professor stuck his nose in and pulled some strings.

But what if I accept it anyway? Should I really care that much how I got the internship, just so long as I did—that I got what I wanted?

I already know the answer: I can't. My pride is at stake here. There's no way I can face Isaac Holmes, knowing what he knows, or sit around sharing ideas with staff who will probably think I'm such a wannabe and will hate every suggestion I make but who will smile and nod and say, "Wow, great idea!" all the while, whispering to each other, "Isaac took her in for Jared Anzler."

Nope. Nope. Nope. I don't want the internship bad enough to cheapen myself for it. If they didn't want me, I don't want them either.

My tears are gone, replaced with an indignant chip on my shoulder. I'm mad at the world, and I'm ready to direct my frustration on anyone who would be unfortunate enough to cross my path right now.

I know I've got to reign in my anger before Harper arrives in an hour or two and especially before I face

Professor Anzler in America Lit class in the morning. I breathe in through my nose and exhale slowly out my mouth, trying to remind myself that Professor Anzler hadn't meant any harm and was only trying to help one of his students. I know in my heart that it was an act of kindness, and I should be grateful instead of wanting to lash out in anger at him. But I wish he would've asked me first before he took it upon himself to make the phone call. I'm sure another student would have fallen all over themselves, thanking him for helping them get their foot in the door at *Evangelism Today*, but my pride is at stake here, and I don't think he understands that.

I have no intention on telling him that though. That would sound so trivial and self-centered. What would I even say? "Oh, hey, thanks Professor for putting in a good word for me, but, um, I prefer to make my own way in the world."

Yeah, sounds lame just thinking about it.

Pushing off the bed, I make my way to my bag and pull out my laptop, knowing I'm about to do something else that's even more lame. I pull the laptop closer and lower myself into a chair, waiting for the laptop to boot up. When it's up and ready, I open my email app and address an email to Isaac Holmes. I don't allow myself to think too much about what I'm doing, or I'll chicken out.

After tapping out an email, thanking Mr. Holmes for the internship offer but claiming that I will not be able to accept it after all due to unforeseen circumstances—like being so lame that my professor has to beg them to take me on—I hit send and snap the laptop closed.

"There. Done. No going back," I say with an air of authority.

But instead of feeling vindicated and relieved, I feel depressed and defeated.

The tears come flooding back like a tsunami.

Chapter Sixteen

IT'S TESSA I CALL TO TELL THE NEWS TO FIRST.

Somehow, I knew it would be that way. I can't tell Mom and Dad that I've walked away from the internship and why. Not yet. They would hurt for me, and I can't handle that level of emotion right now. I'd feel like I need to explain myself and comfort *them*, and I don't have it in me. I'm barely holding it together myself.

Texting or calling Brynne wouldn't be a good idea, because she's studying for finals right now. I'll call her next week.

Anthony is last on the list because I know he'll say all the right words and make me feel better. He's great at that.

Harper already knows because all she had to do was look at my face before cornering me to ask what was wrong. She gave me a great big hug. It was just what I needed in that moment.

So, it's Tessa's voice that I need to hear right now: just the right dose of sympathy with a practical perspective laced with a touch of humor. I tell her the whole story, even the parts she hadn't known about.

"That jerk!" she yells. I pull the cell phone away from my ear. "Why did Anzler have to stick his nose into your business? It was obvious they had no intention of giving you the internship, so why push the issue?"

I'm not sure if her words make me feel better or worse.

"I know, Tessa. I was so mad . . . and embarrassed! Seriously, I feel like an emotional train wreck. First, they reject me, and I'm crushed. Then, Holmes tells me they changed their mind and offer the internship to me. *Whoosh!* I'm on cloud nine and telling everyone I can think of. Then, Anzler throws it in my face—" I stop, take a breath, start again. "Okay, he doesn't *throw* it in my face, but he casually admits that he *put in a good word for me.* Like, gee, thanks but no thanks, Anzler. *Boom!* I'm crashing down through the clouds, hitting the ground, and breaking in a million pieces. Could it get any worse?"

Tessa doesn't answer for a moment. When she does, her voice is calmer. "I'm sorry, Alli. That was wrong in so many ways. You're better than them, you hear me? You don't need them, because something better is in your future. I feel it."

Now that I've gotten it off my chest and received my pep talk from Tessa, I allow the tears to come. "Yeah, I *am* better than them—than *this.* You're right, Tessa."

"I know I am. I always am, remember?"

I laugh. She always knows how to make me laugh. "Only sometimes, Tessa. Don't get a big head. But, yes, this time you are absolutely right. Something better will come along for me."

Chapter Seventeen

Tulane stared out over the crowd, every eye riveted on her, the people hanging on her every word like their next breath depended on it. They adored her, wanted to be like her. If they only knew the truth. That Tulane was not who they thought she was. If they knew, they would cast her out, perhaps even stone her. She couldn't—wouldn't—let that happen. The only person who knew the truth about her was Ravon. He alone had the power to destroy everything she'd built. With Ravon destroyed, her secret would be safe.

I read over the words I'd written . . . and completely forgotten about until now. It's not that Professor Cromwell hasn't reminded us at the end of every class that the first draft of our story is due—I hate to admit that I've pulled a Harper procrastination on this one—in *two days*. The words make for an interesting story hook but not one that I can carry through. It has a fantasy feel to it, and I'm not that kind of writer nor do I even read fantasy novels. But it had been birthed from *something* inside of me, right? Don't all stories originate with their creator?

Like God, our Creator. Our stories all start and end with him. What we do with the in-between chapters is up to us. This Tulane character in my opening. She's hiding something, wanting to appear to others to be someone she really isn't. And she's willing to go to great lengths to make sure she keeps that image. She can't bear for people to know the real Tulane, or they might reject her.

Is that something I'm unintentionally doing? Hiding my true self from others?

No, I don't think so. What people see about me is really, well . . . me. At least I *think* that's what I let them see. But do *I* even know who the real Alli is? Sure, there have been times when I tried to be someone I wasn't—hanging around people I didn't like or doing things I didn't feel good about doing—all with the guise of fitting in.

But I never felt like I needed to *be* someone different with Tessa, Brynne, or any of my friends at church. They've never expected anything different from me than who I am. They knew what I stood for as a Christian, and they still chose to stick around. It was everyone else who made me feel like a misfit puzzle piece.

I'd finally stopped trying to explain to people the why's behind everything I did. "Why do you dress so differently?" they'd ask. "Why do you think you're better than us?"

But I never felt that way—never treated them like I was better. They'd just decided that because I was a Christian and didn't get say or do some of the things that they did, that I thought less of them.

Maybe a part of me is like Tulane: afraid, cautious, preferring to stay in the shadows, wanting someone else to admire her for a change instead of her always feeling like she didn't measure up. But I'm also not that same timid girl anymore.

I decide to continue the story, making Tulane's journey one of self-discovery and acceptance. But there will be no Ravon, a character who's bringing out a dark and ugly part of Tulane I have no desire to pursue.

Alright, two days. Time to shift these writing skills into hyperdrive and write my story.

Chapter Eighteen

I THROW THE LAST DUFFLE BAG IN THE BACK OF MY CAR AND slam the trunk closed before turning to Harper. We look at each other and squeal.

"Eek! I'm so excited," Harper says, throwing her arms around me in a smothering bear hug.

"Me too!" I squeeze back. "If for no other reason than to have a real, home-cooked meal!"

Harper laughs. "You know it, girl! I'm going to gain twenty pounds over break, and I don't care a bit. In fact, between Thanksgiving and Christmas, I'm gonna eat whatever I want!" She gives my arm a playful punch. "Then we can go back to being broke, starving students in January."

"Deal!" I say and give her one last hug before moving toward the car door, anxious to get started on my trip home for Thanksgiving. Well, here at college, they call it Fall

Break, but I'm old school. It's always been Thanksgiving break to me, and that's how it'll stay.

Harper waves as she runs back to the dorm to do some last-minute packing. Good old Harper, always running behind.

I shake my head and laugh as I slip behind the wheel and pull out my phone to start the audiobook I picked out last night. My mom had suggested *The Prayer Box* by Lisa Wingate. She said it made her cry in a good way. Avery was in the room when Mom was talking to me on the phone, and had chimed in with, "No! Listen to Christmas music! It will get you in the holiday spirit!" Mom and I had laughed, and both agreed that there would be no Christmas music until after Thanksgiving. It's a family rule that we celebrate one holiday at a time, but Avery breaks that rule every year.

So, since I wouldn't be listening to Christmas music, and always up for a good cry, I decided to download *The Prayer Box* and listen to it on my trip home.

Once I had the audio book started, I opened a bag of pretzels and set them on my lap before pulling the travel mug of coffee from my bag and dropping it into the cup holder.

I was ready. *More* than ready. I needed this trip.

While talking to Avery on the phone last night, we laughed about something that had happened to her at school last week and how some boy at church was always following her around. "He's so annoying," she complained, while I wondered how in the world my little cousin had grown up so fast in the few months I've been away.

The kid sister I left behind a few months ago, the one who still giggled over fart noises and who loved to do crafts, was speaking a whole new language these days. At eleven, the throes of adolescence are slowly possessing her, and I see that the young girl who idolized me for years will soon move on to more exciting heroes, leaving me far behind. After talking to her last night, my heart feels a little heavier. Like I've left behind a seedling and am going home to a blooming flower.

I'd called Anthony next last night. He and several youth group members were traveling home from an event at another church, and the noise level in the van made it impossible to hear each other. We tried to have a normal conversation for about two minutes before finally giving up and reverting to texting instead.

My mom had invited Anthony to join us for Thanksgiving dinner, and I'd already volunteered us to be in charge of making the mashed potatoes.

I could feel the excitement for home and the familiar building in me with every mile I drove closer to home. I hadn't realized how much I missed the familiar ebb and flow of home.

When the narrator's voice announces, "Chapter Four," I realize I've missed a whole chunk of the story while my mind drifted off. I reach down and hit pause on my phone, and the car abruptly fills with silence. Only the hum of the tires on the road fills the empty space, and I find the sound oddly satisfying, as if the story that had been coming through the car speakers had been more of an intrusion in my thoughts than entertainment.

I allow my shoulders to melt back into my seat while road signs and wide-open landscape race past me and the miles tick by. For about twenty minutes, it's just me and the open road. At one point, a semitruck merges onto the highway, but it gets off at the very next exit. A small town comes up on the right side of the highway, and I notice a large sign with peeling paint and several boards missing. I can barely make out the words painted in red, now faded to pink, *Speedway Skate Rink*. My face warms with a smile. *Tessa*. She loves to skate.

Tessa and I were inseparable. Until last year—the worst year of my life—when things started to fall apart for Tessa, and she pulled away from me. Wow, last year was a tough year. Between best-friend drama, having my heart broken by a guy I shouldn't have been tangling with anyway, and struggling with my faith, I was kind of a mess. That doesn't even count Tessa going through a horrible experience with being trafficked. To our great relief, she made it back home safely after escaping her captors, but she was left fighting demons that only someone who'd been through what she had would understand.

I have some amazing friends in my life—Brynne, who stepped on the scene when things went south with Tessa and gave me a reason to laugh again, and Kristin, a girl at church whom I once considered a nuisance, but I was soon pulled in by her charm—but Tessa will always be my best friend. It's just one of those connections in life that I can't explain. Maybe it's the years of memories through every immature and hormonal stage that girls go through, and that Tessa and I plowed through together that sealed it for us.

Tessa's parents divorced last year before so many other horrible things happened to her, like dominoes plowing in on each other and creating a mass collapse of everything that had been a safe place for Tessa.

I guess if I were to ask her, she would probably say that last year was the worst year of her life too. Not that I'm going to ask her; I'm just starting to see glimpses of the old Tessa, and I don't want to accidentally knock into any more dominoes that might upset her positive momentum.

She's so thrilled to see me this week, and the feeling is mutual. That wasn't the case not too many months ago. I won't get to see her until after Thanksgiving because she'll be at an aunt's house, but we already have Black Friday shopping plans that include hitting up a few second-hand stores or—our favorite—yard sales, if we can find any in the local neighborhoods.

The sun begins to set, casting an orange glow over the open landscape as I pass the familiar landmarks of stately saguaros and ocotillos—with their long, spiny stems—that are native to Tucson, Arizona.

Home.

After seven and half hours of driving, bathroom stops, a quick run through Carl's Jr. for a kid's meal, and another pass through Dutch Bros for a white chocolate mocha to keep me awake, I'm on the last stretch to home. I stare out over the city and marvel at how clean the air here is compared to Los Angeles. It hits me how different my world has been since being in college.

I haven't taken the time to explore past the USC campus, other than to hit a few local bookstores and a trip to Best Buy for a laptop case. And the local public library, of course. I can always count on an interesting conversation with Mr. Library Guy, who I've since come to understand is not flirting with me but who's just a friendly dude with a penchant for winking when he's teasing you. One of these days, I plan to ask his name so I can shake off the Mr. Library Guy title he holds in my head.

When I turn down my street, the first thing that I notice is Mr. Ender's house. Just remembering how Tessa and I tortured the old man over the years by walking on his perfectly manicured lawn causes a giggle to erupt from my lips. We'd get old Ender and his little dog so riled up, you'd think they were defending their property against an enemy army advancing on them. "Poor guy," I say aloud. Maybe I can take a batch of Mom's cookies over to him this week just to make it up to him. If his angry dog will let me anywhere near the porch, that is. Maybe I'll offer *him* a cookie too.

I barely turn the car off when I see Avery's face appear

through the curtains in the window, then disappear. I predict that she's off to announce to the family that I've arrived.

Before I finish tugging my suitcase out of the trunk, Avery is throwing herself on me. I drop the suitcase and lift her off the ground in a big hug. I feel Dad's arm reach around me for a side hug while he reaches down with his other hand to grab my suitcase. Prying Avery off me, I look toward the porch, where Mom stands with her arms wrapped around herself with a smile the size of Texas on her face. When she sees me look her way, she waves but doesn't leave the porch. She knows I'll be in her arms in a minute, so why bother leaving the warm porch? *Smart woman.*

"Alli, you have to check out my new bedspread. It's so cool! Oh, and you'll never guess what color I painted my room!" Avery chatters nonstop as Dad leads the way to the porch and I lean in for a welcoming hug from Mom.

She gives me a knowing look before resting a hand on Avery's shoulder. "Okay, Avery, let's let Alli get settled before you drag her off on a tour of every new change in the house. There will be plenty of time for all that later," she says.

I give Avery's braid a playful tug. "I can't wait to see your room, but you better not have touched anything in my room. That's all I can say."

She shrugs and drops her gaze. "Well, I did sleep in there a few nights after you first left. Don't think it's weird, but, I don't know, it made me feel like you weren't really gone," she mumbles, and I catch a peek at the vulnerable side of Avery behind the preteen persona.

My hand drifts around her shoulders, and I give her a squeeze. "It's okay," I whisper so Mom and Dad don't hear. "I missed you too, sis. Wanna have a sleepover in my room tonight?"

The way her face lights up and her cheeks bunch from her bright smile tells me I could have offered her a trip to Disneyland, and it wouldn't have measured up to the joy she's feeling in that moment. I feel like I've just won the Big Sister of the Year award.

"Girls! Come on in the kitchen," Mom calls out. "I made some hot chocolate."

Now it's my turn to be excited. "With marshmallows and whipped cream?" I ask as Avery and I sprint toward the kitchen. I catch sight of Dad making his way to put my suitcase in my bedroom.

Man, I'm so glad to be home.

For the next hour, Mom, Dad, Avery, and I sit around the kitchen island and sip on hot chocolate. We catch up on the happenings with church, family friends, and Dad's work as a buyer for computer tech companies. When there's a lull in the conversation, Avery jumps in and fills me in on her school and friend drama. "There's these three girls in my class that always give me dirty looks and say all kinds of stuff behind my back," she tells me. "It's all because one of the girls—Stella—thought I was talking about her, but I wasn't! I can't stand them. If Stella doesn't back off, I'm gonna—" Avery catches Mom's pointed look and raised eyebrows that clearly indicate that Avery should reconsider what she's about to threaten to do to Stella.

I don't say a word. In fact, I kinda wanna do some damage to Stella myself. I've been down this road with bullies before, and I know how deep the cuts can go. I've always been protective toward Avery, and a part of me wishes I could keep her from experiencing the painful part of school society, with all its hierarchy and unspoken rules that only the popular kids get to make. But I know she has to do this herself. Avery has to learn when to let it roll like water off her back and when to raise the bullhorn to her lips and call attention to the wrongdoers.

All that Avery's shared with me this evening gives me an idea of what we can talk about during our sleepover tonight. But after my third yawn, I decide that I'll need to put off the big sister talk until tomorrow night. I'm exhausted.

Avery gives me a sympathetic look. "We can save the sleepover until tomorrow night," she whispers. I give her an appreciative smile. "Sounds good," I say.

Mom notices that I'm starting to droop and stands to collect our empty cups. "Why don't you go on and get settled back in your room, Alli? I put some fresh towels out for you in the bathroom. I tried to get Avery to clear her clutter off the counter in there this afternoon, but I can't promise it isn't a mess again." Mom pins Avery with a questioning look.

"Hey!" Avery huffs. "It's totally spotless in there."

Dad stands and walks his cup to the sink, calling over his shoulder. "Enter at your own risk!"

I throw my hands in the air and back out of the kitchen. "Hey, I don't care if it looks like a tornado ran through there. All I want is a hot shower and a queen-sized bed to crawl into. I feel like every time I turn over in that twin bed in my dorm, I'm going to roll right off and onto the floor."

Their laughter follows me as I make my way to my room to unpack.

Chapter Nineteen

I SLEEP LIKE A BABY.

Not the fussy, wake up every two hours baby, but the baby who sleeps so soundly their mother stands watch over them to make sure they're still breathing. I'm about to roll over and go back to sleep, feeling like I could just stay in bed all day, when the faint aroma of cinnamon and bread and a hint of coffee swarms into my nostrils.

I throw back the blanket and hop out of bed. That's pretty impressive since I usually spend a good fifteen minutes browsing on my phone before I get out of bed most mornings. Of course, that all depends on if I've overslept or not. Those mornings, I'm lucky to have time to throw a package of uncooked Pop-Tarts in my bag and grab a vending machine coffee on my way to class.

I forgo making the bed because I want to beat Avery to the bathroom, which shouldn't be too hard, because you have to practically drag her out of bed most mornings. Her door is closed when I pass her room, but I hurry to the bathroom just in case she opens the door and we have to race to be first. I brush my teeth and dress quickly, throwing my hair into a scrunchie. *I'll make the bed and do something with my hair after breakfast,* I assure myself before heading to the kitchen.

Naturally, there's no sign of Avery yet. It's just Mom in the kitchen, setting out butter, syrup, and jelly on the counter.

"What's for breakfast?" I ask, drifting over to the stove to investigate the source of the delicious smell that had lured me out of bed.

"French Toast. Avery's favorite," she says, squeezing my arm as she passes to retrieve plates from the cabinet above the stove. "Where is she anyway?"

"Do you really have to ask?" I say and start pulling silverware out of the drawer.

She sighs and hands me a plate. "Well, help yourself. No sense in waiting for Slowpoke."

I grab the plate with a gracious bow, turn toward the tray heaped high with steaming French Toast, and start forking several onto my plate. "The early bird gets the worm," I say. "More for me!" Then I ask, "Where's Dad?" with my mouth full of bread.

I realize my mistake as soon as Mom cuts her eyes to me. Talking with your mouth full is a big no-no in the Mancini household. However, Mom doesn't even make a face or say a word. Either she's giving me space as an independent woman now or she's resigned to the fact that college has stripped me of my good manners.

"He had to run to the office this morning for a quick meeting," Mom says. She glances up at the clock. "He should be back any time."

Avery makes her appearance just as I'm shoving in another bite of French Toast. She notices me lick the dab of whipped cream off my upper lip. "You made French Toast?" She doesn't wait for an answer but is already taking a plate and making a beeline for the food. She'd taken the time to get dressed—another Mom rule about how we come to the table—but her hair sticks out in several places like an angry dog's hackles. She piles two slices onto her plate and covers them with a blanket of whipped cream.

"Wow, Avery, how about some French Toast with that plate of whipped cream?" I tease.

She looks at me over her shoulder and sticks out her tongue. "I believe I will," she says, tossing her hair and thrusting her chin up with regal flair.

The garage door opening catches our attention. I shove the last bite of my food in my mouth and carry my plate to the sink. Mom reaches for a plate to fix Dad's breakfast.

"I got it, Mom. Dad can just use my plate. It'll just take me a second to wash it."

She nods and moves to put the extra plate away.

A rush of cold air follows Dad into the kitchen. "Happy

morning to my girls!" he bellows, and we ladies turn to greet him with smiles and good mornings in return.

I quickly finishing drying my plate and start to prepare a plate of food for him.

"Is that French Toast I smell?" he asks.

Avery is quick to answer: "You bet! And you're lucky. If you would have gotten home any later, there wouldn't have been any left," she teases.

"Is that so?" Dad grabs the can of whipped cream and holds it over Avery's head like he's about to douse her with it.

She squeals and throws her hands over her head.

Mom and I laugh as I hand Dad his plate, and he leans against the counter so he can talk to us while he eats.

"How about you girls come with me into town so we can pick up some last-minute supplies for baking?" Mom looks to me. "I hear we have another helper in the kitchen this Thanksgiving." There's a twinkle in her eye, and I know who she's referring to.

Heat rushes into my cheeks. "Uh, yeah, we do."

Avery's on it. "What? Who?" She bolts from the table and pushes her head between me and Mom while we wrap up the leftovers. I cast a questioning glance Mom's way, sending the unspoken question: *She doesn't know?*

Mom gives a subtle nod of reassurance, then turns to Avery. "Yes, Avery, remember? I told you Anthony's joining us for Thanksgiving."

The look of shock on her face answers the question.

"You did?" Her jaw drops and her eyebrows shoot to the ceiling as she swivels her attention to me. "*Anthony?*" she says, a huge smile breaking out on her face. "Well, isn't that interesting?"

I pick up the damp dish towel, spin it into a rope, and flick her thigh with it.

"Ouch!" She jumps and yanks the wet dishcloth from where it's hanging over the sink.

I race to the other side of the island out of her reach. "Eww! Don't even *think* about touching me with that nasty thing."

Avery and I laugh and chase each other around the kitchen. Avery even tries to hide behind Dad's chair, but Dad grabs her and holds her while I aim a rather weak flick at her leg. It misses, and I throw my hands in the air. "Truce!"

Avery looks like a truce is the farthest thing from her mind, when Mom walks over and holds her hand out for our weapons. We hand them over.

"Thank you," Mom says. "Now, do you two think you can manage to wash up the dishes without flinging dishwater at each other?" She grins and carries the towels to the laundry room to deposit them into the dirty laundry basket.

I brush by Avery and bump her with my hip, and she shoves her shoulder into mine on the way to the sink. But we're done. Giggling like two kindergarteners, we get to work on the dishes.

Mom ends up dragging us around most of the day. Not

that we mind. We do some early Christmas shopping and admire the Christmas decorations already decorating all the store windows. Avery talks me into trying a boba tea while we're at the Tucson Mall. The first time one of the tapioca balls come up my straw, I almost gag. I race over to a nearby trash can and spit the offending ball into the can. I almost throw the whole drink in with it, but Avery rescues it from my hands and ends up drinking mine and hers.

"That was the grossest thing I've ever experienced, Avery. I'm never going with your recommendation again."

She laughs and follows me into the Apple Store. Mom had gone into the bookstore and agreed to meet back up with us in a half hour.

"I was thinking," I tell Avery, pointing up at a selection of new Apple products displayed on the wall. "Wouldn't AirPods be a cool gift for Dad for Christmas?"

Avery had long ago started calling my parents Mom and Dad too, even though they're actually her aunt and uncle. She never really knew her Dad, so she was happy to assign that title to a male role model in her life. And none of us had expected Avery to call Mom anything other than Aunt Trisha—just like she was never expected to call Dad anything but Uncle Tony—but she told us one time that she didn't want to grow up without a mom, so she wanted to reassign that title to Mom.

My parents didn't mind at all, and I don't mind sharing them with my little cousin either.

Avery pokes a finger on an iPad model screen and

doesn't look up. "Did you win lottery money or something?" she mumbles.

I lean in closer to read the price. The little white card under the AirPods reads $250. "Whoa, guess not," I say. "Weren't they only, like, $130 last year?"

Avery looks up from the screen. "Well, College Girl, you're probably thinking of two generations ago. *Those*"—she points to the AirPods on display—"are the newest deal." She turns back to whatever she was messing around with on the screen. "Maybe check on eBay or something?"

I roll my eyes. *When did this wanna-be-teenager become such a smarty pants?*

"Fine, another flannel shirt it is," I say, giving her hair a playful tug. "Let's go. Mom's probably waiting for us already."

Chapter Twenty

Mom motions Anthony over to where she's leaning over a large roasting pan. Nestled inside is an eighteen-pound turkey covered in a thick layer of butter and seasonings.

"Mom, why did you get that huge thing? There's only going to be seven of us." I count on my fingers to double-check my headcount. "You and Dad, Anthony, Avery, Uncle Marco, Aunt Shelly, and me."

"You know everyone's going to want turkey sandwiches tomorrow," Mom says, popping the lid on the pan and opening the oven door for Anthony. "I'd rather have extra than not enough."

I smile and shake my head before returning to my task of dicing potatoes.

Aunt Shelly grins at me from across the kitchen island, where she works pasta dough in preparation for Dad's homemade ravioli. Even though we have a traditional meal for Thanksgiving, it wouldn't feel like a family meal without some kind of an Italian dish to accompany it. And Uncle Marco had specifically requested Dad's ravioli and homemade sweet sausage. My mouth waters just thinking about it. Along with Mom's homemade red sauce, I'm not even sure I'll care if there's a turkey on the table.

I had tried to get Tessa and her mom to join us for Thanksgiving, but they already had plans to go to Tessa's grandparent's house. Her brother, Aaron, had decided to go to his dad's house, which I know made things tense for Tessa and her mom. I had hoped Brynne would also be in town for the holiday, but she couldn't afford the flight from Florida. I'm bummed, but I get it. Now that we're living like adults and attending college, we're bound to real-life budgets now, even with our parents' help.

Uncle Marco and Aunt Shelly flew in from New York yesterday morning and would be staying for a few days. They're staying in Avery's room, and Avery gets to bunk with me. I don't mind too much, because we like to stay up talking about girl stuff, but Avery snores. And while she blissfully sleeps through her own snorting and rumbling, I don't. I have to nudge her once or twice a night to remind her to roll over on her side.

Uncle Marco is my dad's older brother. He's as loud as my dad is quiet and as obnoxious as my dad is reserved, but I love him to pieces. Whenever Uncle Marco walks into the room, all the attention is on him. He's always singing and bellowing like everyone in the room is hearing impaired and might miss his entrance. On the flip side is my Aunt Shelly. She's the perfect complement to Uncle Marco and one of the sweetest and gentlest women you could meet. She always keeps us laughing with her stories, usually about something Uncle Marco did, all while patting your arm or stroking your hair as she talks. She also makes the best lemon ricotta cheesecake, which I happened to notice she's already prepared and placed on the shelf in the refrigerator.

I can tell that Anthony's already smitten with her and thinks Uncle Marco is a riot. Yet with all the warm, fuzzy feelings of having Anthony and my aunt and uncle together for this holiday, I still feel unsettled. Deep down, I selfishly want my immediate family for myself during these last few days before going back to California. I know with all the festivities and conversation filling every corner of the house, the time will fly by like a tornado, and before I know it, I'll be heading back to college and feeling homesick before I even make it to the end of our block.

I feel Anthony move in beside me just as I'm scraping the last of the potato chunks off the knife and into the large pot on the counter. "Well, nice of you to show up after I've done all the hard work," I tease.

His lopsided grin makes me feel like bees are doing a line dance in my stomach. "Excuse me, My Lady, but I was busy rescuing a damsel in distress."

I laugh, turn the handle of the knife toward him, and

lift the cutting board with my other hand. "Okay, Sir Anthony, how about you carry these to the sink for me? Then"—I point to the large pot full of diced potatoes—"carry this to the sink, fill it with water, and put it in the frig so they're ready to boil later."

He bows low and takes the knife and cutting board. "I shall return shortly."

As I reach for the damp rag I'd brought over earlier and start wiping down the counter, I hear a soft *tsk tsk* from my aunt. I pretend not to notice.

"He's a sweet one, Allisandra," she says. "You know what they say about a young man who sits with your family for a holiday instead of spending it with his own family, right?"

I give in and look at her. "Auntie, he's still going to spend time with his family later tonight."

But she's already shaking her head. "Yes, but he's *here* first."

I push the rag to the side. "Okay, you win. What does it mean?"

The corners of her mouth lift as she leans over the mound of dough in front of her with a conspiratorial gleam in her eye. "He's smitten, my dear." Pointing a white-powdered finger at Anthony, who I notice didn't just carry the knife and board to the sink but is actually *washing* them as well, she says, "You keep that one, Allisandra. He's a good one, and good ones are hard to find." With a final wink, she straightens and goes back to kneading the dough.

"I imagine we'll see him at our table again this time next year." She smiles down at the dough as her hands push and pull at it, so she misses the shocked expression that I'm sure is evident on my face.

I don't have time to think much about her prophetic words before Anthony is back for the pot. Inclining his head with all the formality of a prince acknowledging a peasant, he reaches for the pot, throws his chin in the air, and marches it to the sink to fill with water.

I shake my head and laugh at his retreating back. When I turn to pick up the rag I've discarded, I catch the sly smirk on my aunt's face and pretend I'm going to throw the rag at her.

When everything is prepped and ready for the meal and the turkey is in the oven, we all move to the living room to relax and drink coffee.

"Trisha, don't let me forget to put the lasagna in about an hour before the bird comes out," Dad tells Mom, and she heads back into the kitchen to set a second timer.

"Got it!" She yells back.

Anthony spends the next hour trying to teach me how to play chess, but I keep forgetting which direction each piece can move. "No, Alli, the knight moves in an L shape; he can't go diagonally like that." When I move another piece down two and over one as Anthony had instructed, he sighs deeply. "That's a rook." He tilts his head, and both eyebrows raise. "Are you paying attention? Am I losing you?"

I pucker my nose and give a little head shake. "Sorry, Anthony, I guess I'm just distracted." And I am, because everyone else in the room is laughing at something Uncle Marco's saying, and I'm trying to listen in *and* stay focused on our game, and I'm apparently failing at both.

Not taking his eyes off me, Anthony picks the bottom of the game box from off the floor and lifts the side of the chess board so all the pieces slide into the box. Then, he points to the box lid sitting on the floor next to me.

I give him a sheepish smile and hand it over. "Did I lose?" I ask, trying to make him laugh. I succeed.

He chuckles and takes the lid from me, securing it to the bottom. "Yeah, you lost big time."

We turn our attention to the conversation going on at the other side of the room. Aunt Shelly's correcting some of Uncle Marco's apparently embellished parts of his story.

"No, no, Marco. That's not how it was. It was because you were not wearing your glasses. And I told you to wear them that night, did I not? And the restaurant was dim. It proves that you never pay attention to me." Aunt Shelly wags a finger at Uncle Marco. "You're always here and there, talking and looking at something else. If you paid more attention, *mi amore*, you would not have embarrassed yourself like that."

Everyone's laughing, and I'm dying to know what Anthony and I have missed about this intriguing story.

"Wait," I say and motion for Anthony to join me on the

loveseat closer to the rest of the group. "What happened in the restaurant? I gotta know now."

Aunt Shelly's wagging finger is still in the air, and she directs it at Anthony now. "You, my boy, you make sure you pay attention to that girl when you are out with her." Her finger points at me, then back to Uncle Marco. "This man was the laughingstock of the whole restaurant, I tell you."

Anthony nods solemnly. "Yes, ma'am."

"Well, what happened?" I prod.

Uncle Marco, not one to miss an opportunity to be the center of attention, pipes up. "Okay, okay," he says, waving his hand in the air. "What happened is this. It's true, I wasn't wearing my glasses that night." He looks to Aunt Shelly with one eyebrow arched. "So, I tell your aunt I'm going to the restroom, and that's what I did. Well, when I came out—"

Aunt Shelly huffs and crosses her arms. Her chin lifts as she eyes him.

"Don't you look at me like that, woman." Uncle Marco waggles a finger at his wife and gives a confident nod of his head. "I go to what I thought was our table and sit down. There was a woman seated across from me. What can I say? She had short, dark hair like Shelly." He waves a hand her way. "And this woman had on a dark blouse like the one Shelly was also wearing that night. How was I to know? Her face was behind the menu! Then I hear someone behind me—"

Aunt Shelly interrupts: "I start to *tsk tsk* to him to get his attention, but no! My husband is also hard of hearing, it seems. He is talking to this woman, not knowing that it was not even his wife! How do you not know your own wife?" She throws her hands up and falls back against the couch pillows, shaking her head.

Anthony and I laugh hysterically, not only because the story is hilarious but also because of the antics of my aunt and uncle.

Mom reaches over and gives my dad's shoulder a nudge. "You laugh, but you'd probably make the same mistake."

Dad shakes his head. "Nope. Never. I don't even wear glasses."

Everyone joins in the laughter. We talk for a while longer as we wait for the lasagna and turkey to finish cooking. When the timer goes off in the kitchen, Mom pops off the couch and announces, "Time for dinner!"

As Anthony and I put the chess game away in the closet, he leans close. "I'd never mistake you for another girl," he whispers. "You'd be the brightest star in the room."

I'm still standing next to the open closet with my mouth hanging open when Anthony glides into the kitchen and proclaims, "I'll pull that turkey out of the oven for you, Mrs. Mancini."

Chapter Twenty-One

I'M LYING IN BED WITH AVERY BREATHING SOFTLY IN HER sleep next to me—no snoring yet, thankfully—and I think about the wonderful day with my family and Anthony. Being with him today makes being so far from him most of the time feel even harder.

Is a long-distance relationship worth all this trouble?

I think of all the missing of Anthony, the wishing we could spend time together, the worrying that he's losing interest every time he doesn't call or text, and all the other pressures of trying to date someone over the phone and occasional visits. Then, I think about not having Anthony, not seeing his warm, brown eyes staring back at me from the screen, not hearing him play guitar for me over Face-Time, not listening to him telling me goofy stories to make me laugh . . .

It's worth it. We're worth it.

I look over at Avery and see that she's sound asleep, mouth open and drooling.

Great, she'll start snoring any time now. I roll over and face the wall.

"God," I whisper low enough not to disturb Avery. "What is your will for Anthony and me? I know his future is in ministry, but do I feel that same burden? I clam up every time I even think about inviting someone to church, Lord, much less even *think* about teaching a Bible Study or telling someone about you." A panicked thought pops into my head. "Am I holding Anthony back, God? Should he be with someone, I don't know, more spiritual or who at least has their life figured out? I don't have any talents or abilities that would complement Anthony's ministry, unless you count being able to cook Italian food and putting together a youth newsletter."

I blink back tears. I turn my prayer inward and press my lips together, knowing that if I continue to whisper, I won't be able to keep my crying and voice low enough not to disturb Avery.

It's selfish of me to expect Anthony to wait three more years for me while I finish college. Should I transfer back to Tucson and finish my degree here? I mean, there's no internship in my future here, none that I have the energy to pursue another internship while I'm still licking my wounds after the Evangelism Today *disaster.*

I don't know what to do, God. Show me what to do.

Chapter Twenty-Two

TESSA HOLDS UP A HIDEOUS PURPLE SATIN DRESS WITH A million layered ruffles and huge bell sleeves that, if you wore it to the mountains and got the urge to jump off a cliff, all you'd have to do is spread your arms and hang glide down.

"Okay, that's just ugly, Tessa. And to think that someone actually wore that at one time," I say.

Tessa and I are doing our favorite thing today—thrift store shopping. Tessa just got back in town last night, and when she called me to make plans, thrift store shopping was the first thing that popped in our minds. We've always had that best friend telepathy between us.

We make our way through the aisles, admiring purses and finding some great deals on ugly Christmas sweaters. Tessa even spends several minutes modeling a fur stole for me that she was sure she could make work with a black velvet dress her mom had recently bought for her. I nod approvingly but then point out a small stain on the back. The fur stole is returned to the rack, and we move toward the book shelves, my favorite section in the whole store.

Tessa glances at a few titles but is more interested in the shoes in the corner. She's only gone less than a minute when she rushes over and presses her mouth to my ear.

"Don't look, but guess who just came out of the dressing room?!"

Why do people bother to tell you *not* to look at something when they know that's *exactly* what you're *going* to do?

I look—naturally.

Tessa shoves my head down behind a bookshelf. "I told you not to look! Oh, lord, what if she saw us?"

My head bops up, but the dark hair moving through the crowd near the dressing rooms is no longer in sight.

"No way! Was that Shanice?" I hiss at Tessa, who's practically crawling on my back as I hunch behind the horror fiction section of bookshelves.

A woman pushing a toddler in a cart passes behind us, and I briefly wonder if she thinks we're shoplifting or doing something else nefarious. But I'm too distracted by the Shanice sighting to be overly concerned.

"Yes indeed," Tessa whispers. "That was Shanice, and there's no way I want to see her right now."

I haven't seen Shanice Bradshaw since high school graduation night, when she actually stopped in front of me and my family on the field and said "Congratulations" before moving off toward the mass of people near the bleachers. After luring my best friend into a vortex of slow descent into all kinds of trouble—not that Tessa wasn't a willing participant—and a year of making my life miserable with her uppity cheerleader friends, I almost felt sorry for Shanice at the end of our senior year. She'd stuck her toe over the wrong line and dared to hit on the cheer squad leader's boyfriend, which sealed her eviction from the popular crowd. Suddenly, Shanice saw me for who I really am: a fellow victim and a pretty cool girl. We didn't become friends, but we did form a truce and a mutual understanding of each other after that.

Shanice never even apologized for making my life miserable, but I was past caring by the time graduation drew near and I'd made up my mind to move to California for college and the start of a new life. At least that's what I'd told myself I was doing: starting a new life.

"So do you still talk to Shanice?" I ask.

Tessa is peering over the top of the bookcase, scanning the store for Shanice, when I feel a hard tap on my hip and jerk upward, sending the top of my head into Tessa's jaw with a *thud*.

"Ouch!" Tessa scrambles away from me, rubbing her jaw and giving me an incredulous look, like I'd just hauled off and knocked into her for no reason. Instead of offering the explanation that I thought she'd jabbed me and I was taken by surprise, both our heads wheel toward the girl standing with her hands on her hips.

"I'm right here," Shanice says, eyebrows arched as her gaze bounces between Tessa and me.

Tessa's still rubbing her jaw and looking like she might pass out and collapse on the romance book display behind her.

I'm the first to recover. "Oh, Shanice . . . Hey." I give a quick look around like I've forgotten where we are. "I didn't expect to see you here." I'm not making that up either. A thrift store would be the *last* place I'd ever think Shanice would shop. In fact, I would've thought she wouldn't be caught dead in a place that wasn't Nordstrom or some high-end department store. Old Navy might even be beneath her.

"Apparently," she says. Her lips form a thin, straight line as she shifts to one foot and juts her hip out to the side.

I know Shanice dropped by Tessa's house a few times to check on her after Tessa came home, but I don't know the status of their relationship. I wait for Tessa to take the lead.

Tessa eyes Shanice, but she's not scowling, and the color is returning to her face, so I take that as a good sign. For all the spying and effort she'd put into not being detected, Tessa seems resolved that since Shanice has caught us, so she might as well go with it. "Hey, Shanice. What's up?" Tessa says, reaching for our shopping cart and pulling it closer since it had drifted away in our jostling around. Then, she thinks better of it, takes her hands off the handle and shoves them into her back pockets instead.

Shanice's expression goes from mild irritation to confusion. "Are you guys following me?"

"No!" Tessa and I answer at the same time. *We weren't following you,* I think. *Just spying on you.*

This time, Tessa recovers first. "Actually," she says, pulling her hands from her pockets and resting them back on the cart handle, "Alli and I always come here." She looks to me like she's waiting for my approval before she continues.

"Thrift shopping is one of our favorite things to do." She shrugs. "Oh, and yard sales. Right, Alli?" Her look is pleading, like, *Could you help out a little here?*

First off, I don't know why she's telling Shanice all this. I'm sure Shanice couldn't care less and probably thinks we're just barely above poverty level as it is.

Of course, *she's* here too, so there's that.

"So, what are you doing here?" I ask. I get a look from Tessa that I can't quite interpret, but it doesn't look like she's too pleased with my question.

Shanice surprises me by saying, "I didn't used to come" —her head swivels to look around like she's just realized that she's standing in defiled no-man's land— "here." Her eyes come back to rest on Tessa and me. "But" she shrugs, "my cousin said she finds some really cool stuff at places like this."

Places like this. Yeah, I feel like a lowlife now.

Tessa's head bobs as she considers Shanice's explanation. "Cool. Yeah, so . . ."

I can tell she's fishing for something to fill the super awkward silence.

She looks around as if she's trying to see things from Shanice's perspective. "Um, did you come here alone?" she asks.

"Yeah," Shanice says, offering nothing more. Her eyes narrow. "So why were you two hiding behind this bookcase? And why did *you*"—her gaze sweeps over to me— "ask, 'Do you still see Shanice?'"

I feel my cheeks warm as I clear my throat. "Oh, you heard that?"

It's obvious Shanice doesn't feel the need to answer. She knows I'm stalling.

I look to Tessa for backup, but she's looking at the ground. *Chicken.*

Well, there's no sense in playing this verbal tennis match. It's pretty clear who's losing here. I shoot a dirty look at Tessa, who misses it because—*of course*—she's still studying the fascinating pattern on the linoleum floor. Pulling in a deep breath, I give Shanice my full attention. "Honestly, Shanice, it's more about Tessa and I not wanting you to see us and not the other way around. You know we don't have the best history between us. I mean, I know you and I were cool with each other toward the end of school, but, well . . ." Again, I look to Tessa, but she's staring out the store window now and has pretty much disconnected herself from the conversation. I turn back to Shanice. "I still don't know how to act around you."

Shanice also looks at Tessa, probably wondering why she's not tapping into the conversation. But Shanice's look is dismissive as she turns back to me. "So, hiding from me in public is the best you can come up with? You scared I might attack you or something?"

I tilt my head and consider her words. "Yeah, kinda. Verbally anyway. Can you blame me?" I'm not letting Tessa bow out of this and leave me stranded, so I look right at her now. "I know you and Tessa are friends, so I can't speak for her." I send strong telepathic messages Tessa's way: *Earth to Tessa. Get on board here.*

She gets the message.

Tessa drags her gaze away from the mundane scene outside of an old woman loading her bags into her trunk and gives Shanice her attention. *Finally*, I think.

"No, yeah . . . uh, we're cool. I wasn't really *hiding*. I mean, yeah, I guess I kinda was, but I, uh . . ." She leans her head back, looking up at the ceiling like she's hoping words will sprinkle down on her, then drops her head back down to look at Shanice. "Honestly, I don't know why we were hiding. I guess I just panicked when I saw you."

I fully expect a snarky reply from Shanice or at least a condescending remark, but she looks more deflated than poised for a comeback. "You guys make me sound like a monster," she says. Her eyes are locked on Tessa. "I dropped by to see you after . . . you know . . . to check up on you and all." She looks wounded, and I feel bad now. Shanice and I have never made it past the tolerance stage of our relationship, but she and Tessa *had* been friends. Their friendship may have had a bit of shaky foundation, but they were still friends at one time. But Tessa locked herself away from everyone after her kidnapping ordeal, and no one blamed her for that. At least Shanice made an attempt to reach out to Tessa.

"Yeah, I know," Tessa says. "That was really nice of you. I guess I just thought you were feeling sorry for me or" —Tessa's face flushes before she continues— "that you were digging up information to take back to Kim and everyone to give them all something else to gossip about."

Even I'm shocked at Tessa's confession. Not that I blame her really. I would have probably thought the same thing about Shanice and her snooty friends, especially Kim, the cheer squad leader. In some ways, Kim was worse than Shanice and pretty much controlled every move Shanice and the rest of the cheer team made most of the time. And that included Tessa after she made the cheer team, which had lit the spark that made our friendship go up in flames.

Shanice's expression is grim. "Yeah, well, I guess I can't blame you. Honestly, there definitely was a time when any dirt I could dig up on you would've been used to give me leverage with the group. It's tough trying to stay on Kim's good side." She huffs and shakes her head. "So dumb. I can't believe I cared so much." A sad smile comes across her face. "But I did care because if you aren't one of Kim's fangirls, you're either invisible or you have a bullseye on your back." Shanice looks pointedly at me, and I nod, knowing full well what she's talking about. I had been invisible until Kim and her groupies—Shanice included—decided to mark me with a target.

Shanice turns back to Tessa. "But that's not why I came to see you, Tessa. I'm not that low. In fact, none of the others, including Kim, even knew I went to your house. I really did feel bad about what . . . you know, happened to you and all. You weren't like most of the other girls on the cheer team. You were different. At least you had a conscience when it came to other people." Shanice turns her attention to me. "She didn't know what Kim and Chad and the others were up to with you. Not until everything went down. Tessa even got in Kim's face—and *no one* gets in Kim's face—and told her to stop messing with you. I could tell Kim felt threatened, but she laughed at Tessa and told her to chill out. The next day was when Kim sent that text to Chad."

Yes, the text that sent my world crashing.

I'd been sitting in Chad's truck at a gas station when he went in to buy something. He'd left his phone in the truck, and a text from Kim came through that revealed that Chad was just leading me on as a part of an elaborate prank to see how long he could keep the "church girl" on a string. Naturally, I was devastated and ended up jumping out of the truck and running away from Chad. It was one of the worst things to happen to me in my life. I hadn't known how cruel my peers could be until that experience.

I shudder just thinking about Chad and how Kim and

her friends were in on the prank. A thought stops me as I think about how Shanice is confirming what Tessa had told me all along: that she hadn't known about it. Well, not at first anyway. But what I hadn't known was that Tessa had stood up to Kim for me. All those months, I'd thought Tessa didn't care about me. You don't go from being someone's best friend to acting like they have the plague in just a few months. So, I'd agonized over the fact that being best friends had meant nothing to her and that she'd written me off without so much as a second thought.

So why did Tessa shove me out of her life but then stick up for me with Kim?

Shanice and Tessa are watching me now. They're probably both wondering if I'm about to freak out over the Chad ordeal again. I'm not. Been there, done that already. Besides, I'm not sure if either of them knows that Chad made things right with me before I left and that we're cool with each other. We aren't friends or anything, but I don't feel like I'm going to spontaneously combust every time I hear Chad's name now.

Not knowing what Shanice and Tessa expect from me, I look to Tessa. "Thanks for taking Kim on. I didn't know you'd done that."

Tessa gives a shrug and nods. "I'm with Shanice on that one—even *I* have limits on how low I'm willing to go." She bites down on her bottom lip and looks away.

I know what she's thinking, and I hate it. No matter how many times we've talked about it, I've never gotten through to Tessa that those guys drugging her and taking her that night at the party wasn't her fault. Lots of people were at the party, and it could have been any one of those other girls that night. I know she hadn't made the best choices for a while there and will have to work through some hard things for a long time to come, but I know Tessa well enough to know that she never would have willingly gone off with two guys she didn't even know.

Tessa's words burn into my heart: "Even I have limits on how low I'm willing to go."

Oh, Tessa. You were the victim and had no choice.

"Well, I gotta head out," Shanice says and holds up two belts in her hand. "I better get in line before it gets longer. I have dance practice tonight."

"Oh, you're in a dance group?" Tessa asks.

"No," Shanice says with a hint of humor. "I'm an instructor. I teach the seven to nine-year-olds. I know, me with little kids. Who knew?" She laughs. "Actually, they're super sweet girls, and I really like working with them." She glances toward the front. "Okay, well I really need to get up there. Do you guys want to, you know, hang out some time?" She looks my way. "I mean, how long are you home from college for?"

I look to Tessa for her input, but she motions with one hand for me to answer. "Um, I head back to California next week. Are you available tomorrow? We could do coffee, or . . ." Again, I look at Tessa, who just nods. "You guys can come to my house."

Shanice points at Tessa and starts to walk away. "You have my number. Text me."

Tessa just nods. Again.

I throw my hands up. "What's with all the obliging head nods? Did you lose your voice all of a sudden? I've been doing *all* the talking here."

Tessa steers the cart toward the front. "Come on, Ms. Dramatic. We should get out of here too." She looks back, a wide grin on her face. "Shanice Bradshaw at Alli Mancini's house for a friendly visit. Imagine that. Now I *know* God must be real."

I smack her on the shoulder and brush past her.

Chapter Twenty-Three

Tessa was right.

God definitely must've had a hand in the fact that Shanice Bradshaw is sitting in my living room, chatting it up with me and Tessa like we never had an ocean of issues between us at one time. She's laughing at something Tessa's just said, and all I can think about is all the times I'd wanted to slap that smile off her face. Yet here I am, laughing with them.

Life is full of surprises, I guess.

"Alli," Tessa says, tossing her auburn hair over her shoulder with the back of her hand. "Remember when we dared Aaron to go outside in his underwear and then locked him out of the house?" She bursts out in a fit of giggles, and I join her.

"Oh, my goodness, I'd forgotten about that!" I say.

"Your poor brother. How old was he? Nine? He didn't forgive us for months!"

Shanice covers her mouth with her hand. "No way. That's so mean! Did anyone see him out there like that?"

It takes a second before Tessa stops laughing enough to answer. "Nah, not really. It was pretty dark outside. But you'd have thought everyone in Times Square had seen him the way he carried on when we finally let him back in."

Shanice cracks up and shakes her head. "Almost makes me wish I'd had a brother growing up."

Tessa snorts. "Nooo, you don't. You have no idea what a pain they can be. Consider yourself lucky."

It's my turn to bring up a memory. "Tessa, remember when you talked me into sneaking out of the house to spy on—*I almost blurt out "Chad's party"*—that party, and the neighbor's Rottweiler was barking up a storm?"

Tessa's mouth drops open. "Yes! Oh, wow, that was crazy." She looks at Shanice to explain. I hope she doesn't mention whose party it was either. "We were hiding in the bushes at the back of the house like two psychos. Don't ask me why we thought that was such a good idea—"

"Your idea," I interject.

Tessa rolls her eyes and shoots me a dirty look. "Uh, no one wound a rope around you and dragged you out of the house. You were just as guilty as I was. Nice try." She looks back at Shanice. "Anyhow, like Alli said, this dog next door was at the fence, barking and snarling like he would eat us alive if the fence wasn't between us. We didn't stay long. There was nothing to see but some guy barfing in a planter in the backyard."

Shanice sits wide-eyed. "Whoa, sounds like an adventure. Whose party were you spying on?"

"Someone from school," Tessa hurries to answer, and I'm relieved to hear that we're on the same page. It's likely that Shanice had been at the party that night with the crowd she hung out with, and Tessa would probably be more embarrassed than I would be over the fact that we looked like misfits who hadn't been invited. I keep forgetting that it wasn't long after that night that Tessa was picked for the cheer team, became a part of the in-crowd, and, ironically, became one of the partygoers inside that same house, while I remained an outsider.

Thankfully, Shanice lets it go. "Wow, Alli, I didn't realize you had a daring side. You actually snuck out of the house?"

I ignore the snub. Apparently, she assumes that the few parties I'd managed to end up at were only because Chad had dragged me there. Well, and the one that I'd invited myself to in order to check up on Tessa after being warned by Brynne that there were some shady characters coming that night. Shanice and I'd also had an ugly confrontation that night while I was trying to keep an eye on Tessa and she was determined to harass me, but she was probably too intoxicated that night to remember it now.

Since we're feeling so chummy and none of us have our hackles up at the moment, I feel brave enough to ask the question I've been dying to ask ever since I saw Shanice sitting alone on the bench at school and heard the rumors about her falling out with Kim. "Shanice, you don't have to answer if you don't want to, but . . . well, what happened near the end of the school year? Remember that day when I saw you on the bench and you said everyone had turned on you?"

Shanice looks down at her hands and starts to pick at one of her cuticles. I risk a glance at Tessa, who has a shocked look on her face. I see her lips begin to form a silent question, but Shanice looks up and Tessa quickly drops the look and replaces it with a blank expression.

"Kim made the whole thing up."

I have to work on keeping my own expression neutral now. Like I said, I heard a lot of rumors and trust Brynne's sources, but it's only fair to hear Shanice's side of the story, or at least to be kind enough to let her save face.

She expels the breath out of her lungs, obviously knowing this conversation is going to force her to relive some bad memories.

I almost feel bad for asking now.

"Kim and Alice——" Shanice turns to Tessa. "You remember Alice?"

When Tessa nods, I accept that this was a mutual acquaintance between them. I knew who some of the most girls were on the cheer squad, but I didn't know all the girls' names.

"Well, the two of them started telling everyone that I was messing around with Kim's boyfriend, which totally wasn't true. Her boyfriend knew it was a lie and went along with it to make me look bad."

"Why?" I ask. "Why would Kim do that? Weren't you guys pretty good friends?"

She shakes her head, her eyes closing briefly. "We *were*. But Kim had it in her head that I was trying to oust her from being cheer captain and wanted to take her place. How dumb is that? I couldn't have cared less about being captain. But she was so suspicious and territorial over every little thing. It was only a matter of time before she found something to get mad at me about. All the girls were afraid of her." Shanice looks back at Tessa. "Except you. You never seemed to be afraid of her."

Tessa shrugs. "Why should I have been? Kim was just a princess who was all wrapped up in herself. I only tolerated her, and she knew it. That's probably why she didn't bring me in on the prank with Chad. I can't believe he let her talk him into that. I thought he was more of a man than that."

I have to hold back a laugh at hearing her say that—more of a *man*. Even though it hasn't been that long since graduation, there's just something about being in college now that makes high school and all its drama seem so immature. And I wouldn't consider any of the guys my senior year of high school to be real *men*. All those guys seemed to care about were sports, girls, and parties. I know there were a few good guys—*a few good* men, *ha ha*—that stood above the rest and had good morals and their heads screwed on straight, but my experience was that they were in the minority. Even though I never dated in high school—and I don't consider my naive obsession with Chad a legit dating experience—I'd had a front row seat to many other girls' disappointments and broken hearts and had decided that it wasn't worth the trouble.

Not that guys were chasing me down or anything. Mostly, they just ignored me. Was that my fault? Did I throw off bad vibes that scared them away, or did they just think I was a snob because I didn't play the same flirting games a lot of the other girls did? Well, that and I'm a Christian. That always goes over well in the hunt for common values and virtues in the high school playing field.

But then there was Anthony. He's a guy I *do* share values with, who doesn't play games with my heart, who isn't off chasing other girls and parties. Well, unless it's the Annual Youth Harvest party. Those parties can get pretty wild.

I don't realize I'm giggling until I feel two sets of eyes on me, and Tessa asks, "What's so funny? Are we that boring, or do you have an imaginary friend who's much more entertaining than we are?"

I straighten in my chair. "Sorry, no. I was just thinking about something."

Eyebrows arched, Tessa rolls a hand forward. "And? Do share."

I shake my head. "It was something dumb. Go on. What did I miss?"

Shanice and Tessa exchange a look that clearly indicates they think I've lost a screw or two. "Well, I was just telling Tessa," Shanice says, each word pronounced slowly, like she's speaking to a toddler and wants to make sure she's getting through, "that we should go to the mall this Saturday. I need to get my nails done, and there's a new shoe store that I want to check out."

I'm already shaking my head. "I can't. I'm meeting up with Anthony. It's our last chance to hang out before I head back to California."

I see the puzzled look on her face and explain. "My boyfriend. Anthony." There's still a blank look on her face, so I fill her in. "He's a guy from church. We've been talking for a while."

"Oh, that's cool." She turns to Tessa. "You?"

Tessa suddenly looks like a trapped dog. I know her brain is bobbing for an excuse to not go on Saturday, and I'm not going to be any help. It's not like I'm going to suggest that she tag along with me and Anthony.

I give Tessa a small shrug, which translates to "You're on your own."

"Uh," she starts, then a look of defeat settles on her face. "Sure, um, let me get back to you on that. I'm not sure what I have going on yet."

Shanice leaves a few minutes later, and I turn to Tessa just after I close the door. "Well, that went well."

She lifts an eyebrow. "Yeah, *super* well. What am I supposed to tell her about Saturday? You know I'm not going to go shopping with just her."

"Why didn't you just tell her no?" I move toward the kitchen, and Tessa follows me.

"Oh, right. Just tell her 'Nah, not interested. But thanks for the offer anyway'?" she says.

I grab two Cokes out of the refrigerator and hold one out to Tessa.

She takes it and continues, "I know you were being nice in having her over tonight, and our visit went better than I thought it would, but it doesn't mean I'm ready to hang out with her again."

I still haven't responded when we head to my room. Tessa's spending the night. We're trying to get some extra time in together before I have to go back to college, which I'm *not* ready to think about yet.

Pulling off the tab on my Coke, I set it down on my desk and dig around in my drawer for a pair of socks. "Need some socks? My feet are freezing."

Tessa sits on the edge of my bed, soda untouched in her hand. "Are you even listening to me?"

Plopping down into my desk chair, I tug on the socks and consider my reply. "I don't know. Yeah, I was being nice in inviting her to hang out, and, like you said, it wasn't that bad, considering the history she and I have, but I'm with you. I don't think I'd be ready to go shopping together either. It's easier for me because I'm going back to college and won't even see her again until"—I glance up at the wall calendar above my desk— "probably spring break, and that wouldn't be a priority for me anyway. But I know you don't have that luxury. She's more likely to hit you up to hang out since you're both here."

Socks in place, I grab my Coke and go to sit next to her on the bed. "You know, maybe Shanice needs a friend, Tessa. I know you guys were technically friends before, but that was a different time and under different circumstances."

Tessa opens her soda, takes a sip, then sets it down on the nightstand. She reaches for a pillow and hugs it against her. "I'm not like you, Alli. I'm still learning about God and about what being a Christian is all about and if I'm all in or not. I don't feel as morally obligated as you do to reach out to people. I mean, I know it sounds heartless, but it's not really my problem that Shanice has no friends."

I turn to look at her. "Wow, that *is* kinda heartless. Who says she has no friends?"

Tessa's eyes roll my way. "Think about it. Why would Shanice want to come over here and hang out with someone damaged like me, who clearly has issues to work through, or with you, a girl she taunted for her faith and someone she considered way beneath her station?"

There's a lot I could unpack here, but I choose to focus

on what needs addressing most. "You aren't damaged, Tessa. Not the way you make it sound."

Her gaze drops to the pillow in her arms. "I know. It's getting easier. I'll never feel like the old Tessa, but every day I get closer to feeling normal again. But girls like Shanice don't see the before-and-after profiles or take note of the healing process someone works through to feel whole again. To them, once you're marred, you're damaged goods for life. You know how it is, Alli." Tessa sets the pillow aside and folds her legs into a pretzel shape as she maneuvers her body to face me. "Or maybe you don't. Do you remember when Monica was talking trash about Remi behind her back? And when everyone found out Monica had made everything up and was just spreading lies, no one would talk to her. She was blacklisted by everyone. Even after she apologized, they snubbed her."

"First off," I say, "I have no clue who you're talking about. I remember Monica because she was in your dance class, but the name Remi doesn't ring a bell. Anyhow, that doesn't matter. But when you say *no one*, *everyone*, and *they*, who are you referring to exactly? If you mean the high-and-mighty crowd, I'm not surprised. Maybe she couldn't be trusted and made a poor judgment call, but I would've still been polite to her."

"Of course you would've," Tessa says, dropping her head into her cupped hand. "That's Alli Mancini, always rooting for the underdog. But one: you don't actually know how you would've responded because she wasn't spreading lies about *you*. And two: oh, never mind. You just don't get it."

"What don't I get?" I feel my anger rising. "You hung around with these guys for all of, what, a few months, and now you're justifying their actions? So, are you saying you didn't talk to Monica either? She wasn't telling lies about *you*. Were you just going along with the crowd, which I'm sure I can narrow down to Her Highness Kim? Come on, Tessa. You aren't like that either." I twist my body around and grab the pillow she'd discarded, settling it on my lap and resting my elbows on it while I lean in. "And don't try to veer off the topic of you taking on this damaged-for-life identity. Who cares what everyone else says or thinks?" I reach up and lift her chin with one finger. "What matters above all is what God thinks and what people who love you think. The people who've got your back—not the ones thrusting the knife in it."

There's a sheen in her eyes, and one side of her mouth lifts in a feeble attempt to smile. "Thanks, Alli. I know. You're right. I'm just still trying to convince myself. Keep reminding me, okay?"

I move my finger from her chin to tap the end of her nose. "You know it. I'm not going to let you forget it if I have to tattoo the words *You are loved* on your forehead."

Tessa giggles, and I know we're back on stable ground. She leans back against the headboard and reaches for her Coke. "So, what are we going to do about Shanice?"

"Ha. Correction: What are *you* going to do about Shanice?"

Tessa drops her head back, and we both laugh at the thud of her head hitting the wooden headboard. "Alli! I thought you had my back!"

"I do! In fact, when you two go shopping, I'll loan you twenty bucks to buy yourself lunch. See what an awesome best friend I am?"

Chapter Twenty-Four

I FINISH TYING MY TENNIS SHOE AND SIT UP.

Harper's sitting on her bed, messing with her phone, a look of concentration on her face. Her blankets are crumpled at her feet, and a tower of laundry threatens to topple off the end of her bed. A sketchbook lies open on the floor at my feet. I force myself to focus on Harper instead of the mess around her, or I'll be tempted to nag her about it.

Am I turning into my mother?

The winter and spring semesters have flown by in a flurry of late nights of homework, frozen burritos, Top Ramen, and gallons of coffee. At last, spring finals are next week, and Harper and I have been hermits studying for them. So, when Chloe and Kris invited me to go with them to a local book festival, I jumped on the opportunity for a distraction. I was desperate for a break and thought Harper might be too.

"Last chance, Harper. You're missing out on a lot of fun."

Harper doesn't even look up from her phone. "Can't. Sorry. How hard can this be?" She mumbles to herself.

"What are you doing anyway?" I ask, fishing my Chap-Stick out of my bag.

"Ugh, whatever. This is dumb. I'll just Google the lyrics," she growls, either ignoring or not hearing my question.

I walk over and stand closer. "Earth to Harper. What are you doing?"

She rests her head back against the wall and groans. "I'm creating a new Spotify playlist, and I can't remember the name of a song. Every time I type in a title, it comes up with other song titles that are nowhere close. Even Googling what I can remember of the lyrics comes up with nothing."

"Who's the artist?"

"Clueless," she groans.

"Never heard of them," I say. "Maybe you could just look up one of their albums and go from there."

Harper lifts her head and glares at me. "That's not the name of the artist, Alli. I mean I'm clueless on who sings it."

"Sorry," I giggle. "If it's that hard, maybe forget it for now. It'll come back to you later. Anyhow, are you sure you don't want to come with me?"

Her expression changes to confusion. "Go where?"

Oh, Harper. I adore you, but clueless *sounds about right.*

"Um, the book festival, remember?"

"Oh, the one you're going to with those girls from church?" Her face scrunches as if I've just fed her a spoonful of sauerkraut.

"Yes, the girls from church. We aren't going on a religious pilgrimage, though, Harper—just checking out books and fun stuff. Don't worry, no one's going to badger you to come to church or anything. Come on, just come."

It's not like I haven't tried to invite her to church. I ask Harper every Sunday if she wants to come with me, and she always declines. Sometimes, she offers a lame excuse like "My family's Catholic," as if that will ward off any attempts to convert her otherwise, although I've never seen her attend mass even once since we've roomed together. Other times, she tells me flat out, "No, I'm not interested."

I prefer the latter. At least it's an honest answer.

But I know her well enough to read on her face that she's about to present one of her lame excuses this time.

She looks at the pile of laundry sitting at the end of the bed and sighs. "Nah, I gotta get some laundry done. Plus, I have an essay due on Monday for my Art History class."

I fold my arms across my chest and scowl at her. "Harper, that pile of laundry has been sitting on your bed all week, and I know for a fact you won't start on that essay until Sunday night."

She looks sheepish because she knows I'm right. I'm

always right when it comes to calling Harper out on her procrastination tendencies.

"Fine," she huffs and throws her feet over the side of the bed. She stands and shakes out her left foot. "Ouch, my foot's asleep."

"You'll come?" I say, hope fluttering in my chest.

"No," she says, avoiding looking at me, reaching for her phone on the bed instead. "I'm going to get started on that essay."

I try not to let my disappointment show. I bet my last dollar Harper won't touch the essay or her laundry while I'm gone. I lift my chin and attempt to act haughty and playful, even though I'm bummed out. "Fine. Stay locked in your dungeon with your boring old essay and clueless-whoever if that's what you want. I'm going to have a fun day exploring books and eating funnel cakes."

Harper hobbles over to our mini refrigerator and pulls out an orange juice. "I don't even like to read, Alli, so I'd be bored to death anyway. Might as well get some homework done."

I could keep sparring with her over this, but I resist the urge, letting it go. But there are some things I *can't* resist. "Well," I say, swinging my bag over my shoulder and nodding my head toward the pile of dirty clothes. "You might as well get some laundry done while you're at it."

I guess I *am* like my mother.

Chapter Twenty-Five

CHLOE AND I BROWSE THE DYSTOPIAN BOOKS ON DISPLAY.

I have several set aside in a stack at the end of the table, but I'll have to narrow down my selection to match my budget. I'll stick with borrowing many of the books from the library rather than owning them. It's not like Harper and I have room for books in our dorm room anyway. The few I brought from home have been relegated to under my bed to leave room for the textbooks and supplies we need for our classes.

I hear Chloe bust out laughing and look up to see Kris making her way toward us, loaded down with a cardboard box filled with books. "What in the world did you do, girl?" Chloe asks. "Did you leave any books for anyone else over there?"

Kris replies with a cheesy grin and a little happy dance as she balances the box between her hands. "My favorite fantasy author's whole series, signed by the author! I couldn't resist!" she bellows, and everyone around turns to stare.

Chloe shakes her head and walks over to offer her assistance, mumbling something about Kris tripping over a rock and dumping her beloved books into the dirt. She peeks into the box, which is still firmly in Kris' grip. "Wait, don't you have all these already?" she asks.

Kris smiles down at her treasures. "Yes, Ma'am, I do. But these are hardbacks, and mine are all paperbacks. I'll trade those in at the used bookstore. Besides, did I mention that the author signed these copies?"

I make my way over, clutching the two books I'd dwindled my own choices down to. "Yes, Kris, I do believe everyone at the festival heard you."

The three of us share a laugh.

I hold up the two books in my hand. "I'll be traveling lighter, so you'll have plenty of room in your trunk on the way home." I glance back at the book table. "I gotta pay for these real quick." I make my way over and hand a twenty-dollar bill to a girl who looks to be about fifteen or sixteen and who's wearing a floral dress and denim jacket. "Cute outfit," I say as she lowers the books into a paper bag.

"Thanks!" She says, handing me the bag. "Hope you enjoy the books. The third in the series comes out next fall."

"Oh, good to know! Thanks!"

Kris, Chloe, and I walk out to the car to deposit Kris'

heavy box, then spend the next two hours walking around the book festival, stopping to listen to an author book reading and picking up a few children's books for Chloe's twin nieces. We stop by the food court and have corn dogs and French fries. Before we leave, I spy a vendor selling funnel cakes. I'm not the least bit hungry, but I told Harper I'd be eating funnel cakes today, and I have to keep my word, right? I end up sharing one with Kris and Chloe.

By the end of the afternoon, the three of us are sweaty and sunburned, and our feet hurt. But we'd all had a great day browsing and buying books and just hanging out together. I was glad I'd come.

Harper would've had fun too. As we head toward the parking lot, I tell Kris and Chloe that I want to look over some art books before we leave to see if I can find one for my roommate.

"Is she the girl you tried to talk into coming today?" Kris asks.

"Yeah. She claimed she had stuff to do, but honestly, I think she's scared we'd gang up on her and try to convert her," I say.

Chloe leans in, lowering her voice so only Kris and I can hear. "Maybe we would. We'd back her into a corner and keep her hostage until she repented of all her sins. Then, we'd make her promise to keep the sister oath."

I punch Chloe's arm. "Sister oath? What in the world is that?"

Chloe shrugs. "I just made it up. It sounded cool."

Kris grabs us both by the hands and tugs us toward the parking lot. "Okay you two. I'm over this place. I have a blister on my right heel, it's hot out here, and one of us has BO. Not that I'm naming names; just saying."

Perfectly synced, Chloe and I both say, "It's you," before breaking into a fit of giggles.

Kris lets go of our arms and shoots us a dirty look. "Okay, okay. I see how it is. You two can find your own way home. Wouldn't want you being offended by my offensive odor all the way home."

All it takes is one look from Chloe and we bust out laughing again. Even Kris can't resist joining in.

It was such a great day.

Chapter Twenty-Six

I FROWN DOWN AT THE SELECTION OF ITEMS IN MY CART: A case of Dr. Pepper, cherry Pop-Tarts, a box of granola bars, a small jar of creamy peanut butter, and a box of Cheez-Its. My favorite go-to snack is Cheez-Its and peanut butter, which everyone in my family thinks is gross, and tell me so every time I eat it in front of them.

Well, they aren't here now, are they?

I look again at all the junk in my cart and feel instantly guilty, so I steer toward the produce section and toss a bag of apples into the cart. *Healthy snack; check.*

I'm third in line and browsing through a *Women's Health* magazine—ironic, I know, as I'm leaning on a cart full of junk food and one guilt-assuaging bag of apples—when my phone buzzes in my purse. I pull it out and see that it's my mom calling. The line shifts forward, and I'm next, so I decide to ignore the call. I can't get caught up in a conversation with my mom when it's almost my turn to pay. I silence my phone and drop it back into my purse.

I'll call her when I get back to my room. She's probably just calling to ask if I've gotten over to Best Buy yet.

She gave me a laptop case for Christmas that's super cute, but the zipper is broken. Instead of Mom exchanging it and having to mail it out to me, she gave me the receipt so I can just exchange it at the Best Buy near me. I haven't gotten around to it yet though.

Back in my dorm room, I unload my bags, stacking the Dr. Pepper and apples in the small, college refrigerator before racing to the bathroom since there'd been no public restrooms in the store.

When I come out, Harper's dumping her backpack out on her bed and spreading the contents all over her comforter. It's obvious she's in a panic, searching for something.

"What's up, Harper?"

She doesn't look up but grabs a pouch and unzips it, overturning it onto the bed with everything else. "I've got ten minutes to get to class," she says, her voice coming out in a whine. "I can't find it. What did I do with that stupid thing?" She starts pulling out old receipts and cards from her wallet before shaking out a few coins from a zipper section. She groans before tossing the wallet on the bed.

"Whoa, what did you lose?" I ask, my eyes searching the scattered items on her bed even though I have no clue what we're looking for yet.

"My thumb drive," she says, throwing up her hands. "I have an essay saved on it that I was planning to print in the Student Services building before class, but I can't find it. *And* I'm going to be late to class now!"

It's on the tip of my tongue to ask why she doesn't just use a cloud service to store her documents and to point out that thumb drives are outdated, but I know that's not going to help her situation and will only send Harper into further panic-mode.

"Okay, okay. Calm down" I say. "Let's think this through. Where did you see it last?" I ask, glancing around just in case Harper set it down somewhere else in the room.

"I had it during my first class this morning," she says. "Some guy behind me offered to share his notes, and I handed him my thumb drive to upload them on."

I swallow down another remark about outdated thumb drives.

"He was going to email them to me, but I told him to just put them on my drive."

I can't help myself. "Why? Email would've been way easier."

She doesn't answer but starts digging through her pockets.

"Yes!" She holds up the small, black drive and throws her hands in the air. "Thank you, God."

"Well, glad to see God was first on your list of credits. Have fun cleaning up that mess," I say, pointing at the chaos on her bed.

From across the room, my phone chimes again.

"Oh, I forgot about Mom!" I scurry across the room to my purse and snatch the phone out. Mom's face is on the screen as I tap the accept button and put the phone to my ear. "So sorry, Mom! I forgot to call you back. I got your call when I was in line—"

"Did you get my voicemail?" Her voice is soft and timid, like a child asking a question they don't want to hear the answer to.

I pull the phone down and look at the screen, thumbing down the notification bar. I see that I have three missed calls and a voicemail. I press the phone back to my ear. "No, I didn't. Sorry. I set my phone down and got busy helping . . . well, never mind. Um, is everything okay?"

There's nothing but silence on the other end, and now I *know* that everything is definitely *not* okay.

"What's wrong, Mom?"

Silence.

"Mom . . . what is it?"

From the corner of my eye, I see Harper sit down on the edge of her bed, her arms full of the items from her backpack. Her attention is on me, and it's as if time stands still as I turn and lock my eyes on her, instinctively reaching for the lifeline I know she's sending my way.

"Mom?"

I hear her pull in a shaky breath before she speaks. "Honey, it's—" Another long sigh. "It's . . . Brynne."

I make it over to my bed and lower myself onto it—my

eyes never leaving Harper's. "What about Brynne? What happened? Is she okay?"

Harper turns and releases her burden back onto the bed, then comes over to sit next to me. I feel the brush of her fingers on my elbow.

"No, Alli. It's not . . . okay. There was an accident. She and a friend were on their way back to the college from a study group meeting. A truck driver . . . I don't know, they think . . . they think he fell asleep at the wheel—"

"Mom, stop! What are you telling me? Is Brynne alright or not? Is she in the hospital? Where is she?"

"She's gone, Alli. I'm sorry. She . . . Brynne and, um, her friend, well, they . . ." A soft sob escapes before she can finish. "They were both . . . gone . . . at the scene. There was no way, with that truck crossing over the line—"

"*Gone?!* Mom, are they . . . is Brynne, *dead?*"

Harper's arms are around me, but her presence barely registers as I collapse against her. I push a fist against my mouth, holding back the scream I feel bubbling up my chest and into my throat. A wave of shock and horror rushes through me, making me shake so hard I feel like I'm going to throw up.

Harper presses closer. If she wasn't here, I know I would've already slid to the floor.

Mom is sobbing so hard that I barely make out the words. "Yes. Oh, honey, I'm so sorry. Yes, they're gone."

She can't even say the word dead. I don't know why that's

such a big deal to me in this horrible moment, but it's like I need to hear her say it. Like it's not real until she does.

"Alli?" Mom's voice reaches for me across the miles. Her voice is wobbly but stronger. "Alli, listen. I don't want you to be alone right now. Is Harper there?"

I don't answer but just shove the phone against Harper's chest and throw myself down onto my pillow. I can't hear what Harper is saying into the phone above the screaming and wailing in my pillow.

Why God? Why? No! No! No! Not Brynne!

I feel hands rubbing my back and hear Harper's soft voice, but I can't hear what she's saying. I'm only aware of my ears thrumming with the sound of my own heartbeat, the flood of despair pressing down on me, and the wet, snot smeared into my pillow and across my cheeks.

I'm drowning and suffocating all at once.

Harper gently nudges my shoulder. "Breathe, Alli. Just breathe."

I don't know how long I lie there, lost in grief and pain, my world collapsing around me, sucking me into a tunnel of misery.

Sometime later, Harper strokes my hair and presses my phone into my hand. "It's your mom, Alli. Talk to her." She helps me sit up, and I press the phone to my ear.

"Alli. It's me," Mom says. "Dad and I are coming to get you. We'll be there in a few hours, okay?"

"No, Mom." My head is throbbing, but I'm thinking clearly enough to at least make this one decision. "I need to be here for classes. The new semester just started, and I can't . . . I just can't leave right now. I'll be okay. Let me know when you have more details, and—"

"Honey, listen to me. We don't want you to be alone with this right now," Mom says.

I glance down at my pillow, tempted to sink back into my tunnel of misery, but manage to keep myself upright. "No, please don't. I'll be okay. Honest."

Oh, God, how will I ever feel okay after this?

"I just need some time to process this, Mom. As soon as you have information about arrangements . . ."

It hurts to swallow. To breathe. To think.

I can't believe I'm having this conversation right now. "Just keep me updated when you know more, okay?"

Mom spends the next few minutes trying to change my mind, or maybe she's just trying to convince herself that I'll be alright, until Dad takes the phone away from her.

"Allisandra." His deep voice is soothing but commands a strength that I need more in this moment than Mom's excessive worrying. Tears flow again as I imagine Dad's warm eyes looking at me, filled with love and concern.

"Dad, what happened?" I don't know why I'm asking again. I know Mom told me all they knew, but I just need to hear it from my dad, as if the authority he commands will help seal the news into my heart. My brain is all cried out, but I have no clue how my heart will handle the news when it truly sinks in.

"We really don't know everything yet. Brother Terrell called to let us know. He'd just gotten off the phone with Brynne's father and was on his way over to their house."

Dad blows out a long breath before continuing. "Anyhow, it's just like your mother said. Brother Terrell told us that Brynne and one of her friends from her study group were driving back to the college when a truck drifted over the median and into their lane. It was a head -on collision, and, well, the other girl in the car was transported by ambulance to the hospital, but she passed away as they were wheeling her into the emergency room. Brynne was . . . she was pronounced dead at the scene. The driver of the truck . . . well, we know he was also taken to the hospital, but that's all we know. Brother Terrell doesn't know the driver's condition at this point. Oh, Alli. I'm so sorry, *tesoro*."

My chest fills with emotion at the mention of Nonna Mancini's term of endearment for me. "Tesoro," she'd tell me in her gentle voice whenever I whined to her about something that seemed unjust and unfair in my life. "We don't always understand the Lord's ways," she would tell me, "But we can trust that his plans are always for our good. Besides, he doesn't have to explain himself to us." Nonna had a way of making you feel corrected but completely loved at the same time. What I wouldn't do to have her arms around me right now and to smell the scent of her skin.

"Oh, Dad, this is awful." I choke on the words. "I feel

so helpless over here, like I should be doing something. But I wouldn't even know what to do if I were there."

"I know, Alli, that this would be so much easier if you were surrounded by people who love you. Your mother and I hate that you are dealing with this news alone. I know your roommate is there and that you have a strong church group for support, but it's not the same as family. Are you sure you don't want us to come get you? Even just for a few days? I'm sure your professors would understand and would make a way for you to catch up on assignments."

I shake my head, even while my heart cries out, *Yes!*

"No, Dad. I'll just take the day off classes tomorrow. I promise. I know I won't be able to focus, and I need some time to think and be alone. But I'll need to be back in classes after that, if for no other reason than to stay busy and distracted. I'd only fall apart if I came home, and I can't afford to do that right now."

I look over at Harper, who's sitting on her bed watching me intently, her face a mask of concern, and lift a hand to reassure her that I'm making what I feel is the best decision, even if I still need to convince myself of that. She nods and assures me with her sad smile that she completely understands. I'm grateful for her support right now. I know she'll give me all the space I need without me even asking. I turn my attention back to my conversation.

"I want to save coming out there for when a decision is made about, you know, a funeral . . ." I almost choke on the word, "or whatever her family decides."

Another flood of tears threatens to overwhelm me, and I drop my head to my chest, letting the silence on the line linger. Dad doesn't press me.

When I've taken a few breaths and can manage to talk again, I continue. "How's Brynne's family, Dad? Is someone with them? Is the church, you know, organizing anything?"

"Yes, yes, they are," Dad says. "The ladies at church have already started putting together food deliveries, and Pastor is at the house with Brynne's parents. Sister Karen, the ladies' leader, will be sending out texts and making phone calls to let people know any new details and what kind of support the family needs. As soon as Mom and I know anything, I'll call you. I promise. Okay, hon?"

I brush at my cheeks with my sleeve and stand, walking over to the window. I look down at the stillness below. No students race down the sidewalk to class or lounge on the grass, talking with friends or quietly reading a book. Nothing to distract me while I wade through the deep waters of grief and questions exploding in my brain like grenades.

Dad and I talk for a few more minutes, and he assures me once again before we end the call that he'll contact me as soon as he knows something. "In fact," he says, "I'll call and check on you tomorrow either way."

"Okay, Dad," I whisper, letting my forehead rest against the cold window glass. "Thank you. And . . .Dad?"

"Yes, sweetheart."

"Pray for Brynne's family, okay? And me. Pray for me, Dad."

"We will, Alli. For everyone who's hurting right now, we're praying."

Chapter Twenty-Seven

My eyes are fixed on the ceiling, the glow of the nightlight next to the bed casting long shadows from the fan blades across the room.

I've just talked to Tessa on the phone for over an hour. We cried together and comforted one another, and, somehow, Tessa found a way to make me smile before we hung up. Tessa wasn't as close to Brynne as I was, but she still feels the loss and hurts for me as well.

I hardly notice the tear trickling from my eye until it tickles my ear. I roughly brush at it. A sob rises in my chest, bubbling into my throat, until I feel that it's about to suffocate me. The words of Pastor Fischer at Grace Center from Sunday replay in my head: "God loves you. Even when you feel like your world has been shattered in a thousand pieces. When you're hurting and nothing seems to make sense anymore. God's love remains a steady force in our life that nothing can destroy."

The anger in my heart burns like hot acid. "I don't want to feel like this anymore, God," I cry out into the empty room. "I've always known that you love me, but I've never really known what that meant. And now that I am hurting so much, I want to know. I want to feel what your love can do for me because I can't bear this pain right now. I was following all the rules and being a good girl—at least the best that I could be. I thought that's all you required of me: just toe the line and stay out of trouble. That's all you want, right?"

I'm sobbing now, and I don't even try to fight it. In fact, the harder I sob, the better I feel. Like a wall of concrete is crumbing from the top down, one chunk after another cascading to the ground.

"What do you really expect from me, God? What could the God of heaven and earth *need* from inconsequential Alli Mancini? I used to spend so much time worrying about fitting in and being accepted by others, but I guess I never stopped to consider if you accepted me and if your plan for me was my priority or if I was following my own agenda."

The sobs soften to hiccups as I force myself to focus and try to tune in to the voice of God, just in case he's trying to get a word in while I pour out my complaints. I'm probably being the sincerest I've ever been in my life, and the moment feels so intense that I half expect God's audible voice to fill the room.

No, let's not do that, God. That would freak me out.

Taking deep breaths to settle myself, I feel a calm come over me, and a peace I haven't felt in a long time fills every pore of my body. I realize I don't need an audible voice. God's voice rings clear and true in my heart, and I embrace the love that God reveals to me as I open my heart to him.

"I've never had to measure up to anyone but you, God. I see that now. And that's enough. *I'm* enough."

Confirmation that I know hasn't been manufactured by anything on my part floods over me like a soothing river, and I lift my hands to God in worship and absolute surrender. In this moment—just me and God with no outside distractions—my heart is no longer troubled, all my questions seem unimportant, and my pain dulls. I feel nothing but an incredible sense of peace, and there is nothing that seems more important than this moment with God.

I don't know how long I lie there, speaking no words but saying volumes in my spirit. I'd been so angry with God for taking Brynne that I never stopped to be grateful that she came to know him before he called her home. Brynne was ready. And if I don't let go of all the bitterness I've been wrestling with, I'll be the one who isn't ready to meet God. I wouldn't want to meet God with all the ugliness I've been wearing like a badge that I was positive justified my accusations against him.

My mind goes to Job in the Bible. If anyone was justified in being upset with God, it was him. His loss was staggering, and there was no relief in sight. I would've cried out to the heavens with my complaint just as much, if not more, than Job had. But, even in Job's justifiable state, with a strong case against wrongful treatment, God comes to him and corrects him—even chastises him. *Ouch.* But Job takes it like a man. He swallows his frustration and humbles himself before God.

I don't think I could do that, Lord. I really don't.

But, thankfully, I'm not Job And although I may have felt very far from God as Job did for a time, not once has God forgotten or left me. I didn't believe that an hour ago, but I think I do now.

My eyes well with tears again, but this time with gratefulness and trust in God.

"I'll see you on the other side, Brynne."

Chapter Twenty-Eight

My phone comes alive with the song "You've Got a Friend in Me," my message notification for Tessa that I reinstated after deleting it last year during our "rough patch," as my mom likes to call it.

I hurry to silence the notification.

Several people in the library shoot me incredulous looks, like I've just given away their position in a hide-and-seek game.

Sorry, I mouth to the onlookers, but most have already turned their attention back to their books or computer screens.

I peek down at the screen to read the message from Tessa. It's just two words:

Call me.

No emojis. Just a short sentence. So unlike Tessa.

I glance around and spot an exit door at the back of the library. I almost hate to give up my table because it was the last unoccupied one when I arrived twenty minutes ago. Since then, the library has only gotten more crowded. *Oh, well; I'm done here anyway.* I look at the book on the table that I'd been reading and chew on my bottom lip. It's a romantic comedy, and I'm actually really getting into the story. It's not something I would've normally picked up to read, but Professor Cromwell had challenged us to find a book outside of our go-to genre, and I'd decided to try this one. I hate to abandon it.

I glance once more at the exit door and shake my head. Picking up the book from the table, I grab my backpack and make my way to the front desk.

I'll check this out and call Tessa as soon as I get outside.

I set the book on the counter and dig in my bag for my library card. I find the card shoved behind a punch card for a local coffee shop and pull it out. It isn't until I slide it across the counter that I notice the clerk is the friendly Mr. Library guy again. He's holding my book in his hands and wearing a huge grin on his face.

Does this guy get tickled over everything?

"Hmm, this is different," he says. He holds the book a little higher, just in case I might've not noticed he was holding it. "*Falling Head Over Feels?* Kinda off from your dystopian taste, isn't it?" He looks at the cover, then back at me. "Interesting title, though." He studies me a moment. "It's Allisandra, right?"

Thankfully, there's no one around to witness my embarrassment this time, but I still shrink down into my T-shirt a little. "Yeah, well, it's for a class. The, um, professor wants us to read something we wouldn't normally read. So, I, uh, thought it looked like a fun read." I take a breath, gathering the courage to finally ask. "And, by the way, how do you know my name is Allisandra? My library card says Alli."

He grins and turns to dig through a pile of notes on the desk behind him. After a few shuffles, he pulls out a white sheet and sets it down in front of me. When I pick it up, I see that it's a receipt for two of my college textbooks, and it has my full name printed on it: Allisandra Mancini.

"You left it in one of the books you returned." He points at the paper in my hands. "I wasn't snooping, honest. I was planning to give it back to you but forgot last time you were here."

He runs the scanner over my book and then scans my card. Picking the book up, he hands it to me. "Well, you'll have to come back and tell me if it was a fun read or not. I'm not into romance myself, but I'd love to hear your take on the story." His lopsided smile gives away that he's messing with me.

I pull the book toward me and tuck it into my bag. "Rom-com," I can't resist adding. I don't know why I care, but I just can't let him believe I'm some flighty girl who lounges around reading shallow romance books.

"Excuse me?" There's a confused look on his face, so I enlighten him.

"Romantic comedy," I say. "Not just any dime-store romance book." I point down where the book is nestled down in my bag. "This is a clean rom-com book—no hanky-panky, weird stuff going on, you know . . ." My cheeks grow warm, and I can't for the life of me figure out why I'm continuing this conversation with a guy, library clerk or not.

Awkward.

His eyes light up. "Oh, I know what rom-com is. And, right, you're not into shady, weird stuff. Got it." He gives a curt nod, steps back from the counter, and shoves his hands in his pockets, like he and I are just having any normal old conversation, which we're not.

"Okay, then," I say. "Have a good night." I'm done with this conversation, and I have a phone call to make.

I'm barely out the double doors when I pull my cell phone from my pocket and tell Siri to call Tessa. It rings once, and I hear Tessa's voice croak out, "Hey."

I trot down the front steps of the library and start scouting for a private place to talk. My options are endless because there's a ton of huge trees and benches, and there's no one out here. I make my way over to the cleanest bench and lower myself down, sliding my bag off my shoulder but keeping my arm tucked into the handle. You can never be too cautious of purse snatchers.

"Hey. You sick? You sound like you have strep throat or something."

She's silent for a moment before answering. "No, I'm not sick. Do you have a minute? Are you alone?" Her voice is low, and there's still a noticeable crackle to it.

"What's wrong, Tessa?" Now I'm worried. That's no strep throat. She's upset. *Oh, Lord, I can't handle any more bad news right now.* "Tessa?"

"I didn't think I was going to have to testify, but now they say that I do." Her words are rushed and panicky. "I don't know if I can do it, Alli. It's just too soon. I don't want to face any of those guys in court."

My shoulders droop, and it feels like all the air has seeped out of my lungs. "No. Oh, Tessa, I'm sorry. I thought—"

"Yeah, me too. But they never found the other girls that escaped with me that day, and if I want to see any justice done, I'm the only one who can make it happen. And I do want that; I *do* want to see these guys put away for life—or worse, I don't care—but why do I have to be the one to do it? They were trafficking girls, Alli. Lots of them. They couldn't find anyone else?"

I breathe deeply, trying to settle myself so I can stay in control for Tessa's sake. It's my turn to be there for her, and I can't let my own feelings about this run away from me.

Be strong, Alli. Tessa needs you.

Tessa told us that she and two other girls had escaped the place where traffickers held them and that they'd gotten separated after that. Tessa called the police from a payphone, but she didn't know what happened to the other girls.

Then, the three guys involved in drugging and taking Tessa had been discovered when they'd showed up at another party, where they were assumed to be scoping out more victims. They must not be talking or giving up where they brought the girls and who they were working for. Tessa's obviously the only witness the prosecutors have, and her testimony is vital to the case.

Although she'd tried to give the police as much information as she could about where she'd escaped from, it was the middle of the night, and she and the other girls had just ran, not paying attention to their surroundings as they fled for their lives. And when Tessa had been taken there originally, she'd been drugged and had no way of knowing the exact location. The police searched the area in the direction where Tessa pointed out she'd run from, but nothing had turned up suspicious.

I hear Tessa sniffling, and I know the news is causing her a great deal of anxiety, but I'm proud of how strong she's being. I tell her so. "Tessa, you're amazing, and I'm so proud of how strong you're being. I know that this is going to be hard and that you might feel like you're going to have to relive a lot of bad memories you'd prefer to leave buried and never have to deal with again. You've worked so hard to overcome and heal from what you went through, but I want you to know something."

Tessa remains quiet, and I hope she's not shutting down on me.

"Are you listening?"

"I'm listening," she answers with a shaky voice.

"Your testimony could put these guys away, Tessa—hopefully for a very long time. And, when the police uncover more details or get these scumbags to talk, you'll be helping other girls find their way to freedom and possibly preventing many others from becoming victims. That makes you a hero in my eyes, Tessa."

"What if I don't want to be the hero, Alli? Remember how I felt when I first came home and everyone was analyzing me and trying to get me to talk about my experience? It made me mad. I felt like I was always being observed for signs of depression or being interviewed for a future episode for some show on Netflix. I wanted everyone to just leave me alone so I could work through things on my own and talk when I was ready to talk, even if that was never."

"It's not good for us to work through those kinds of things on our own, Tessa. You know that."

I didn't need to remind her that she hadn't been too successful with it either. Instead of healing, Tessa sank into a deep depression for a while, and her parents worried they might have to intervene by force.

But she'd come through eventually, and that was only after months of therapy and—the most effective of all, in my opinion—spiritual counseling. She'd started coming to church with me and, although she digested things in her own way and in her own time, found purpose and an inner calm that helped her blossom into a stronger, more resilient version of Tessa. She still wasn't ready to return to school to finish her senior year, preferring to finish her studies at home, but I think that was a good thing. The only people that surrounded Tessa during that time were positive, encouraging influences. And her school friends—mostly the popular, shallow types and the farthest thing from true friends—were into partying and shady stuff that had partially been responsible for Tessa's troubles to start with.

"Yes, I know." Tessa's voice reigns my thoughts back in. "I guess I'm just panicking. Everything was just starting to feel normal for me again. What happened to me is still the first thing that hits me every morning, but when it does, it doesn't hurt as much as it did. Does that make sense?"

I'd long ago decided that I wouldn't even try to pretend that I knew what Tessa was feeling or what she was going through. I promised to be a good listener and always have her back, but I would never know—by God's grace—what it felt like to live through what she had.

"I think it does, but you're the best judge of this, Tessa. If you truly can't go through with testifying, then you tell them how you feel. Advocate for yourself. But I want you to at least promise me that you'll think about it first—even pray about it if you feel comfortable doing that—before you give your answer. I'll be praying too. Okay?"

"Okay. I can do that." There's a calmness in her voice that hadn't been there a few minutes ago.

"How's everything else going?" I try steering the conversation to more shallow waters, trying to get Tessa's mind on something else. "Are you still thinking about college?"

Tessa and I had always planned to attend college together. When we were kids, she'd already known that she was going to become a veterinarian, while I waffled between being a journalist or wandering aimlessly through life with no ambition. Luckily, I chose the former.

Tessa fanned the flame of becoming a vet and kept it burning all the way through middle school and high school. She never wavered from her dream, and it was always something I admired about her.

We had it all planned out too. Tessa, the smart one with all the top grades, would allow me to be her lowly roommate who would probably barely make it into college so that she could be there to prod and push me through to a degree.

Then, things started falling apart at home. Her parents divorced, her brother, Aaron, started acting out, and life became a weight that she struggled to carry. She sought validation and a thrill to take her mind off her trouble and tried out for the cheer team, something Tessa wouldn't have normally cared anything about. Then she made the team. There was nothing bad about that, except that it proved to be the finger poke that sent the line of dominoes tumbling down, sweeping her away with the momentum. Not in a positive direction either.

It didn't just affect Tessa but me too. What should have been the highlight of our teenage years became a nightmare for the both of us as we drifted apart and came close to hating each other.

But here we are, on the other side of the storm that tested our friendship to its limits. Not that we came out unscathed. We both bear some battle scars that will stay with us for a long time. And, what really hurts, is that now I'm off pursuing that college degree . . . alone. The one predicted to be the least likely to be successful and the one between us who cared the least about a higher education, off to college while Tessa crawls her way back to a normal existence and works up the courage to believe in dreams again.

"Actually, I am considering college. I mean, I *was*—"

"Tessa, no. These people already stole too much from you. It's time to take back your life."

There's a long pause, and I wonder if she's heard me. Then she answers, and I sense a new strength behind her words. "Yes, you're right. I *am* going to college. I don't know why I'm letting this get to me so much. I've already started looking into taking classes at the University of Arizona. They have a veterinary science program that looks pretty good, and, of course, it's close to home. Mom and I even worked on my FASFA a few nights ago, and I plan to apply for financial aid."

"That's my girl," I say.

Tessa chuckles softly, and I feel the tension in my chest ease. Her anxiety levels may raise again tomorrow, but she's okay right now. One day at a time.

"You know," I continue, "Harper and I could probably fit an air mattress on the floor between our beds if you want to come to USC."

"Yeah, right, as if I could even if I wanted to. Besides, I could never live that far away from your dad's three-cheese ravioli."

"What?! Dad made three-cheese ravioli? When? They invited you over for dinner? This is *so* not cool." My dad makes the best ravioli in the world. He and Mom cooking together is one of the things I miss most about home. When those two are in the kitchen, you know it's going to be a gourmet five-star-restaurant meal.

"Actually, your parents invited me *and* my mom. But . . . it's not until this next weekend. My mom's making two desserts to bring too."

I groan. "Don't tell me. Key lime pie?"

Tessa laughs. It's good to hear her laugh, but I'm honestly jealous over here. "Yes, and blueberry cobbler with vanilla bean ice cream," she says.

"Seriously, Tessa! Just stop! I'm so mad right now!"

"*Well*, you're the one who decided to move away. I'll FaceTime you when we go over, and you can watch us eat. How does that sound?"

"If you do, I'll never speak to you again."

"Liar." She snorts.

I have to laugh too. It's either that or cry.

"Thank you, Alli. I needed this talk," Tessa says, all joking aside. "How about you, Alli? Are *you* doing okay?"

I know she's talking about Brynne, but it's a topic I don't want to talk about. Not yet.

"Today, I'm okay. Ask me again tomorrow. You might get a different answer."

Chapter Twenty-Nine

I'VE LEFT THREE MESSAGES SINCE YESTERDAY, AND HE HASN'T called me back.

That in itself isn't a huge deal; we all get busy sometimes. But something similar happened last week. We had planned to FaceTime around 5:30 when he got home from work Monday night like we normally do, but when I called, it went straight to voicemail. Again, not a big deal. It happens. But Anthony didn't call me back the rest of the night, and that *never* happens.

When we do finally talk, I get the sense that he's distracted and a little impatient to get off the phone. I shared something amusing that happened in one of my classes, and he just answered with, "Ha, that's funny."

It felt so insincere.

Then, when I tried to ask his advice about a class I'm thinking about taking next semester, he brushed me off with, "I don't know, Alli. You're the one in college. What do I know about college classes?"

He apologized right afterward for snapping at me, but the damage was done. I was hurt, and it just added to several other hurts that were all connected to Anthony recently.

"I think Anthony's growing tired of me," I told Tessa on the phone one night. She told me I was probably reading too much into Anthony's distraction and said I should tell him how I feel. "I'm sure there's an explanation for how he's acting, Alli," she told me. "He might have a lot on his mind right now, or you just caught him at a bad time."

Caught him at a bad time?

Like I'm supposed to just respond with, "Oh, so sorry that every time I call, I'm catching you at the wrong time. Perhaps you'd like to hit me up when life has chilled and the timing is better for you? Maybe you could pencil me in when you don't have so much going on?" Is that what I'm supposed to tell Anthony?

I pick up my phone and try once more. When he doesn't answer—*again*—I drop a major hint about how I'm feeling in a voicemail: "Hey, Anthony, guess you have things going on. Give me a call when it's convenient for you." I do my best to keep the sarcasm out of my tone, but if a tiny bit creeps in, well, that can't be helped. I'm not going to sit around like a puppy waiting for its owner to toss it a bone. I can make myself busy too.

In fact, Harper and I have plans to go see a play the

college drama department is putting on tonight. Neither of us have a lot of extra money to throw around, but the drama department needs audiences to practice in front of, and it only costs five bucks to get in, so Harper and I always make it a point to go when the opportunity comes up.

I set my phone to silent and jam it down into my back pocket.

As usual, Harper is running late. I try to start prodding her at least ten minutes before we go out together, so she has time to recover from not being able to find one of her sandals or from hunting down a scrunchie for her hair, which inevitably always happens. But I'm distracted with thinking about Anthony's silence lately and what's really going on with him. It's not like him to brush me off like this, and I feel my heart starting to splinter a little more each day.

I don't get it, either. Anthony's not the type of guy to drop hints that he's losing interest. He's too much of a gentleman and too honest. He'd just tell me. And at least that would be easier to take than the silent treatment or whatever avoidance tactic he's using.

Is he afraid of hurting my feelings? Would this be his first time breaking a girl's heart? It's not like it's my first time getting my heart broken, although I'd describe my experience with Chad Barton last year as pretty heart-shattering. But Chad had only been toying with my heart anyway. Anthony's been nothing but sincere and honest with me since we started our relationship.

So why won't he talk to me now?

Harper's tinkering around, looking for something in her nightstand.

I glance at my watch. We should have left five minutes ago. "Harper, you ready? We gotta get going."

"Yeah, just looking for a—"

I roll my eyes and reach for the elastic band on the table next to me. Stretching it between my fingers, I fling it toward her, and it lands on her pillow.

She reaches for it. "Oh, perfect! Thanks!" she says and starts to wind her hair up into a high ponytail while moving toward her purse, which is sitting on the chair.

I lean over and grab the purse. "I'll carry it. Finish your hair. Let's go."

"What's the play we're seeing tonight again?" I ask, handing her the purse as I turn back to lock the door.

Paper crinkles behind me, and I know Harper is looking at the flyer she must have pulled from her bag. "Uh, let's see. Agatha Christie's *Murder on the Orient Express.*"

"How appropriate." I snort, thinking about how I'd like to strangle someone right now.

"Huh?" Harper says.

"Nothing," I answer, slipping the key into my bag.

Chapter Thirty

"BREATHE, TESSA."

Her body remains rigid next to me.

I lean in closer. "Are you breathing?"

"Um, kinda," is her brief response.

I sneak an arm around Tessa and discover that she is, indeed, breathing, but she's breathing too fast. "*Deep* breaths, Tessa. Slow it down."

"Would you make up your mind?" she hisses.

She's tense and a nervous wreck. But I don't let her irritation affect me. In the courtroom today, she'll face the men who kidnapped her and put her through hell. She won't have to testify yet, but just seeing them again is going to be hard for her.

I feel her body tremble against me, and I want to walk into that courtroom, shove my fist into her tormentors' faces, and ram my fingers deep into their eye sockets.

How dare they hurt my best friend.

But I keep my emotions in check because, honestly, I'm trying to help Tessa keep hers under control at the moment. She needs me to be strong right now. But so help me, if just one of those two scumbags looks at her or me, I'm going to . . .

"Alli."

Tessa lays her head on my shoulder and grabs my hand. Her fingers are icy cold. "Can you pray for me?"

The image of doing bodily harm to her tormentors fades as I redirect my focus on Tessa's needs right now. I can rage and be carnal later. Right now, she needs me to tap into the spiritual part of me.

I have to admit, it's hard. I'm not feeling all that spiritual at this moment. But pulling in a deep breath, I try to change my frame of mind and not let my thoughts remain in a dark place. I realize that it's not just Tessa who needs a touch from God. I need strength too.

I pull Tessa closer and rest my chin against her hair. I try to rein in my thoughts and focus them on God. I close my eyes, and my lips move silently as I start by asking God to forgive me and to help me have the right attitude as I bring Tessa's needs before him. I feel peace like a warm breeze sweep into my heart. But just before I begin to present my petition for Tessa to God, her voice interrupts me.

"Out loud," she says.

My eyes fly open. I'm not sure what she means.

"I'm sorry, what, Tessa?"

"Out loud," she repeats. "Can you pray out loud?"

I bite my lip because I've never prayed out loud in front of anyone else, unless you count saying the blessing over a family meal. But I nod my head, her hair brushing against my chin, and begin again.

"God, I bring Tessa before you . . ."

Chapter Thirty-One

It's been a grueling few weeks for Tessa and her family.

I agonize over the fact that I can't be with her for all of this. I was able to be there for the first day in court, but I'd only been able to sneak away from classes for a few days. Thankfully, my parents made arrangements for me to take a train from Los Angeles to Tucson, and that took a lot of pressure off me driving and was a much faster trip.

I've questioned myself a thousand times about why I'd thought that I just *had* to go to college in California instead of attending the community college closer to home. I know all the reasons I *thought* I had to, but none of them carry any weight against everything that's happened back home since I've left: Brynne's accident, Anthony pulling away, and now Tessa going through this trial without me being there with her. Sure, Tessa calls me every night and updates me on the day's events and the progress of the trial, but it's not the same. I want to be *there* with her and go through this with her in person, not just offer second-best support over a phone conversation.

Tessa was called up to testify on the third day of the trial, and I told her I would be praying and fasting for her on that day. That's a big deal for me, too, because fasting is my least favorite thing to do. But I really wanted to get God's attention and knew that fasting would keep me focused on praying for Tessa's strength.

And I think it helped, because she was holding herself together pretty well after the ordeal was over. After that, Tessa kept tabs on the trial from home and was available for any additional questioning without having to show her face back in the courtroom. Although I knew it was one of the hardest things she'd ever had to do, there seemed to be a measure of peace for her that came with testifying and knowing that she was finally getting some justice for her pain.

We talked on the phone for a while tonight before she said she was tired and was going to head to bed. I was thinking of doing the same thing when I get a text from Anthony:

> Hey, you busy? I thought we could catch up.

From the way my heart flutters when I read that, I realize how much I've been missing Anthony. The focus on

Tessa and the trial has been an effective distraction, but it hasn't completely blocked out my sadness that Anthony and I haven't talked in a few days and how that seems to be happening more and more lately. Yet I don't want to let on how much it bothers me and want to come across as casual and unaffected as possible. Basically, I don't want my wounded pride to be too evident. I text back:

> Sure! No FaceTime for me, though, if that's cool. Give me a few minutes. I'll call.

Five minutes later, after several deep breaths and a quick pep talk to calm my nerves, I call Anthony back.

Normally, Anthony and I prefer to FaceTime because it makes us feel more connected to see each other's faces, but that's not an option for me right now because I'd been cleaning our dorm room before I hopped on the quick call to Tessa to check up on her, and I look like I haven't showered in a week. My hair's in a messy bun that's more on the messy side than a bun, and my T-shirt collar is stretched and frayed. The last thing I want to do is give Anthony another reason to question whether he wants to still pursue this relationship.

He answers on the first ring, which is a good sign. "That was fast," he says in a cheerful voice.

I find myself smiling in spite of the hurricane of doubts spinning around in my head. *Had he picked up on the sarcasm in the last voicemail I'd left?* "Yeah, I just needed to take care of something really quick." Naturally, there's no way I'm telling him that I'd needed to give myself a pep talk just to get the courage to call.

"It's cool. No problem. What have you been up to today?" His voice sounds so relaxed that I can picture him sitting on the recliner in his room—*Only Anthony would have a recliner in his room*—doodling on a sketchpad, with an energy drink on the desk at his side. I hadn't realized until we started getting to know each other better that Anthony loves to draw and is pretty good at it. He's always showing me his sketches of airplanes and old trucks when we FaceTime. He says that drawing relaxes him and that, besides his mom, I'm the only one who's seen his "doodlings," as he calls them.

"Nothing exciting," I say. "Just cleaning and burning off some nervous energy. I've been working on an essay for my American Lit class for the last three days, and my eyes were starting to cross."

There's a soft chuckle on the other end of the line, and it feels like there's never been any dead space between us. The familiar and comfortable that we'd shared before settles back over us like a favorite blanket.

I take a deep breath and lower myself onto a chair. I must have been stressed because I hadn't noticed I'd been pacing the floor until just now.

"Yeah, I know what you mean," he says. "It feels like I haven't had time to breathe here lately with all that's been going on. Of course, I don't have any extra surplus of nervous energy like you do. In fact, most days I don't have any energy left at the end of the day."

This is news to me. Anthony never mentioned anything to me about having stuff going on, and I wonder why that is. "Oh, wow, really? What's been going on?"

"Just all the stuff that needs to be done with Brother McGuire before next month."

I'm still clueless about what he's talking about. Brother McGuire is our youth pastor back at my church in Tucson. Anthony's been assisting him for the past few years, and there's always some activity, event, or service that Anthony lends a hand with. "What stuff needs to be done before next month?" I ask. "Is there a youth conference or something coming up?" I'm pretty sure my mom would have told me about any church events coming up. She keeps me filled in about everything happening at church, especially since she and Dad usually have their hands in most things there. Then again, maybe she did tell me, and I'd just tuned her out.

Anthony is silent for a moment. When he does answer, I sense the hesitancy in his voice. "You know, uh, next month. When I take over as youth pastor. Don't you remember?"

It's my turn to take a moment to answer. "Brother McGuire is stepping down? You're taking over? Uh, no, I didn't have any idea. When did this get decided? My parents haven't said a word and . . . you never said anything either."

"Oh, wow. I'm so sorry, Alli." I hear the regret in his

voice. "Actually, most of the church doesn't know yet. It hasn't been announced or anything. Brother McGuire plans to tell the youth next week, and then we plan to have a youth rally where it'll be formally announced. That's what I've been busy helping him plan." He pauses. "I really didn't tell you? I thought I had."

"No," I answer numbly. "You didn't tell me."

"Huh. I guess I must have been more distracted than I thought." Anthony clears his throat and announces with an air of formality. "Alli. I am hereby informing you that I will be taking on the role of Youth Pastor at Tucson Apostolic Church in the next few weeks." He finishes with a laugh, "There, now you know."

I make an attempt to laugh too, but it comes out sounding more like I'd tied a scarf too tight around my neck. "Wow. That's, uh, great. I'm happy for you."

"Thanks," he says. "But, again, I'm sorry, Alli, for leaving you hanging."

"It's alright, Anthony. Really. So . . . is that why you've been so quiet lately? You've been, uh, working on prepping for this youth leader transition?" I try to keep the hurt out of my voice. I really do. I don't want Anthony to detect that I've been feeling neglected.

"I've been quiet lately?" He asks it less like a question and more like an admission of what he knows is true.

"Kinda."

Lame, I know. I'd prepared to say a whole lot more than

kinda, and I wonder where all the words went that I'd rehearsed a hundred times in my head.

Filling my lungs with air, I'm determined not to let things go on like this a moment longer, and I'm ready to bolster my piddly one-word answer with a diatribe of all I've been obsessing over lately about our relationship, when Anthony jumps ahead of me.

"I'm sorry, Alli. You're right."

I feel the pin of his words push right into my lungs, causing them to deflate, with all their pompous air and lofty words, into useless, shriveled balloons. I have to take another breath just to refill them.

In fact, even the words I'm about to say with that second breath flee again.

The third time's a charm, I think, and try to muster up a fresh batch of determination to spew out my complaints.

Again, Anthony beats me to the punch. "I've been wrapped up in myself lately, haven't I? I mean, I've been so pumped up about this transition into youth leadership and focused on wanting to make sure I do everything just right before coming on board and taking on this responsibility that everything—and *everyone*—has been pushed to the side lately. My mom even made a comment at dinner tonight that it's the first time we've sat down to a meal together for a few weeks."

I open my mouth again but then close it, waiting to see if Anthony has anything else to add before I speak up.

He does.

"I don't know, Alli. All this busyness and trying to make an impression. Am I letting pride get in the way?" Again, I open my mouth to speak, but he continues. "I guess I knew in the back of my mind that I was putting you on the back burner too, but I told myself that you were busy with classes and homework anyway and could probably use the space."

I twirl a loose strand of hair that had escaped from my messy bun and consider what I want to say. I wasn't expecting anything that Anthony's confessed, and now I find myself rerouting my words—and my attitude.

"I don't know about pride and misguided intentions, Anthony," I say, "but you're wrong about one thing." He doesn't prod me to go on, but he doesn't need to. "I don't need any space. When we talk, it's actually a welcome distraction from all the pressures of college and the mind-numbing boredom of this matchbox I call my dorm room. Other than talking to you, the only exciting part of my week is going to church and Harper's lame jokes."

I'm relieved to hear him chuckle because the conversation is starting to feel too heavy for me. Anthony is obviously feeling guilty and asking for my input, so the last thing I want to do is make him feel worse.

I make an attempt to lighten the mood. "You can take up all the space you want in my life," I say, then realize how completely cheesy and sappy that sounded.

"You got it, Alli." He sighs. "I really am sorry. I didn't realize how tied up I was with all this and that I'd hurt you.

Next time, send me a text or something and remind me that I'm being a jerk. Deal?"

"Deal." A smile splits my face in two, and I feel like a girl with a schoolyard crush. I'm almost giddy with relief that we've dragged the elephant out of the room and cleared the air between us.

"So," I say, then notice the unnatural trill of my voice. I clear my throat and start over. "So, tell me more about this leadership position. Do you think you're ready for it?"

Anthony doesn't hesitate. "Yeah, I think so. I've always felt a burden and a passion for working with young people —you already know that. Sure, I have to admit, I'm a little nervous about the extra responsibilities that come with the role, but I've prayed about it and really feel like I'm in God's will." He sighs deeply. "There are a few things that will be difficult for a while, like counseling the girls and all —Sister McGuire will still need to step in for that—but I'll leave the details up to God. I'm ready for whatever he wants for me."

I'm not sure what to think of the comment about things being difficult for a while because I get the feeling that Anthony is referring to the fact that he doesn't have a wife to support him. He didn't come right out and say it, but it's obvious with his comment about the girls who need counseling and guidance. It wouldn't be appropriate to counsel with girls alone, which I wholeheartedly agree with, but what's a guy to do when he's unmarried and finds himself in a youth leadership position with a female youth member who needs help? I guess he'd thank God that Sister McGuire can step in when she's needed.

I don't say all this to Anthony, deciding to focus on a smaller detail. "You aren't that much older than most of the youth, Anthony." I chuckle. "Will they have trouble respecting your authority?" But I already know the answer. Anthony has always been respected, even admired, by the youth at church. Brother McGuire has given Anthony lots of opportunities to lead at youth events and to speak at youth meetings, and you could just tell the youth think that Anthony walks on water, and they've always been willing to help out with whatever he asked of them.

Sure, there were a few rebels in the group who had it out for any authority figure and would've bucked against the twelve disciples themselves, but most were good kids with sincere hearts. And some of the rebels came around with maturity, though there were always a handful that you needed extra patience and grace for.

That's another area Anthony excelled in: he had loads of patience and was always willing to spend time working with the youth who needed the attention. In fact, in the spiritual department, Anthony was, well, everything you could want in a youth leader.

"Never mind," I say, breaking out of my thoughts. "I know they've always respected your leadership. You could tell some of them to jump off Sentinel Peak, and they'd do it. I think most of them consider you a leader in their life already. You'll just have a little more authority now to put that leadership into practice. Congratulations, Anthony."

"Thanks, Alli. I really appreciate that. I know there will be challenges, though. Up to this point, even though Brother McGuire put me in charge of things from time to time, most of the guys still considered me one of them. When it came to discipline or reprimands, that came straight from the boss—not me. Now that I'll be their youth pastor instead of "one of the guys," their perspective of me will probably shift, and they might pull back. In fact, I'm almost positive they will. I think I might even find myself lonely for friendship in the future."

"Well, then, I guess you're stuck with me," I say, and we both laugh.

Anthony and I talk for another twenty minutes about random stuff: the latest crushes in the youth group, his mom's new car, my classes . . . all the *normal* stuff. It feels so good knowing that everything is cool between us and that our relationship is still intact.

Before we hang up, Anthony hesitates a moment before saying, "I'm sorry I made you feel neglected, Alli. No, let me rephrase that. I'm sorry I *did* neglect you—neglect us. I really care about you and never meant to make you feel like I don't. I just got distracted and took advantage of the fact that you'd be there when things settled down. Maybe I shouldn't have assumed—"

"It's okay, Anthony. Honest. I'm not going anywhere. I don't mind being Rapunzel in her tower, waiting for her prince to show up and rescue her from her prison of boredom."

That got a belly laugh out of him, and I break out in giggles. It's like I'm a lovestruck middle schooler or something. The thought sobers me. *Love?* Where do Anthony and I go from here? Is that the next level for us: love? I think about my recent conversation with God—a conversation that was more about me crying and feeling sorry for myself, as usual—and wonder again, *Where do I fit into all this? Into Anthony's ministry?*

When do people know if things are deepening between them? Do you just go along enjoying each other's company —well, over the phone for us anyway—and share things you wouldn't trust anyone else to know, then feel like you can't breathe without hearing their voice, and then. . .and then? Is there some point you come to where you're ready to say goodnight but the words *I love you* come out of your mouth instead?

At first, my crush on Anthony snuck up on me like a blast of wind out of nowhere. But after months of talking and only seeing each other face to face when I go home on breaks, I find myself waiting anxiously for his calls and feeling little tickles in my stomach when his smile reaches through the phone screen and brushes across my cheek. It's that intense sometimes—as if he's really here in the room with me. And, yet it never feels like enough. I want to hold his hand, to smell his cologne, to hear his breathing . . .

Wow. How did we get here? Or, I guess I should ask:

how did *I* get here? I haven't asked Anthony how he feels directly. How *would* I ask? "So, Anthony, do you ever have a hard time swallowing because your mouth goes dry when our eyes meet? Do you ever get an overwhelming urge to immediately call me back within seconds of us hanging up because the silence feels so unbearable? Is it just me?"

"Alli?" Anthony's voice snaps me back to attention. "You still there?"

I empty my lungs, nice and slow so he won't detect that I've been holding my breath. I'm thankful, once again, that we aren't doing a FaceTime video so he can't see that I've been off in a dreamland.

"Yeah, I'm here." I let out a sigh that turns into a yawn.

"Well, that's my cue. I can take a hint."

"Oh, stop it," I mutter. "It's a yawn. I'm not snoring or anything."

"Hmm, I don't believe you," he says, but I hear the teasing in his voice. "I guess I'd better go anyway. I have to run an errand for my mom before she gets home."

The urge hits—the one to call him back—and we haven't even hung up yet. "Okay," I mumble, sadness trickling through every cell in my body. I don't want the call to end. A tiny speck of reckless impulsiveness pokes at my chest, and I almost say the three words just to try them on for size, but reason swats them back down to reality.

"Goodnight, Anthony," I say responsibly and sanely.

"Goodnight, Alli."

Chapter Thirty-Two

I THOUGHT I'D BE AN EMOTIONAL MESS, OR AT LEAST CRY A whole lot more. But it didn't turn out that way. Oh, my throat clogged up, and my eyes burned with unshed tears several times, but I never totally broke down. In fact, the tears that threatened in the background during the entire service were tears of joy more than sorrow.

I know why too.

Brynne's memorial service—or homegoing as we prefer to call it at church—was a beautiful event. From the choice of music, all inspirational songs that Brynne loved, to the PowerPoint slides that showed photos of her from childhood and growing up, to the people who spoke of her life and of what Brynne had contributed to them, everything was so well done and uplifting that I couldn't help but smile at the peace I felt inside.

I look around the fellowship hall where the church

ladies have poured their love into preparing a wonderful meal for Brynne's friends and family. As I watch the ladies bustle around, refilling cups of iced tea and slicing and serving pie, I feel such a gratefulness in my heart to belong to such an amazing family of God.

A family that included Brynne.

My eyes drift toward the heavens, where I imagine my friend dancing on golden streets of glory. In fact, I might even feel a tinge of jealousy that Brynne is already in the presence of God, while the rest of us are longing for that day. Not that I'm anxious to expire any day soon, but part of my heart is already invested.

I'll see you again, my friend.

I think back to when I first met Brynne. She and I sat at a table together in science class, along with a guy named Zach. Brynne and Zach were the brainiacs between the three of us—not to mention that Zach was also a meticulous notetaker whom I relied on way more than I should have—while I was barely passing and, more often than not, missing one or more of the materials needed for the class. Between the two of them, they carried me through science and Mr. Martin's notoriously detailed (and boring) lectures.

Back then, Brynne and I were also both being harassed by Kim and Shanice. They didn't just mess with us in class either, but they messed with us every chance they got outside of class too. Kim and Shanice had apparently decided that Brynne's style didn't meet their standards, and me being a Christian girl made me the perfect target for them as well. The whole awful experience put Brynne and me on common ground that ended up leading to a meaningful friendship. We needed each other.

Or maybe I just needed her.

Yeah, I think that was it: I needed Brynne more than she needed me.

When Brynne started coming to church with me and became a Christian, our bond deepened. Although Brynne could never fill the empty cavern that Tessa had left in my life, her friendship was definitely a healing balm. God had known just what I needed at that point in my life.

I feel an arm wrap around me and draw me in close. I look up to see Sister Vickers, a sweet, elderly lady in our church.

"How are you doing, sweetheart?" She lowers herself into a chair next to me and fixes me with warm, brown eyes that are flanked by deep creases at the corners. Her dark skin is flecked with age spots and a map of tiny cracks, but her smile melts away the years.

She squeezes my hand between hers, and I answer with a nod, not sure I trust my voice enough to answer. I was doing fine until she asked that question, but now, seeing the compassion and concern in her eyes, I feel like I might melt into a puddle at her feet.

"Would you like me to get you something to eat, dear?" she asks.

My gaze drops to her bent, arthritic hands as they surround mine in a tender embrace—hands that have lovingly served others for more years than I've been alive. I know her offer of food is her way of showing love.

How many plates of food has this sweet lady served in her lifetime?

When I lift my head, I see the shimmer of unshed tears in her eyes. I'm so moved that this precious lady hurts for me when I know that she's lost a son and a husband herself.

"How do you always know just what I need?" I ask her, smiling with tears in my own eyes. "Yes, I would love something to eat." I'm not really hungry, and I don't know how I'll get the food past my lips, but I wouldn't deny Sister Vickers this offer of love even if I have to choke the food down.

Not only does Sister Vickers shuffle back with a plate heaped high with potato salad, fried chicken, green beans, and something red and jiggly that resembles Jell-O, but she sits down next to me, watching over me like a mother hen.

I make a show out of taking small bites out of most everything—avoiding the red blob—and smiling at her like I've never eaten a better meal in my life. Apparently satisfied that I'm getting adequate nourishment, Sister Vickers gives my hand one last pat and makes her way back to the kitchen to join the other ladies.

I set the fork down the moment she's out of sight, thankful to be alone with my thoughts once again. I'm emotionally drained. Brynne's memorial service had been delayed until a time when most of Brynne's friends and family could be here. I'm glad because the delay gave me time to work through my own feelings and mourning privately before having to confront them in front of a bunch of other people.

Many of our friends were here today. including Tessa and Kristin, but they hadn't wanted to stick around for the meal, claiming they weren't hungry. I hadn't wanted to either, but I hadn't felt up to driving myself here today and had come with my parents, and they'd stayed.

I glance over at the table where Brynne's family sits huddled together, talking in quiet tones. We'd already shared hugs and tears earlier, and I want to give them space now. My mom peeked my way several times today to check on me, and I managed to give her a reassuring smile each time just to keep her at bay. But what I really want to do is go home, crawl under a pile of blankets, and have a good crying session all alone in my room.

I know that it gets better from here. That time heals all wounds. But I'm not quite there yet.

Almost. But not yet.

Chapter Thirty-Three

"ARE YOU DOING ALRIGHT, BESTIE?" TESSA ASKS, SITTING AT the other end of the long couch. If I were counting, I'm sure that would be at least the hundredth time someone has asked me that question since Brynne's memorial service this week.

Tessa looks good. Her auburn hair is fixed into two long braids that hang down past her shoulders, and her cheeks glow with health. But what stands out the most to me is that her smile appears genuine, not forced, as it had been many months ago.

Tessa has always turned heads and been admired for her looks. She'd always taken care of herself and was determined to keep her nails manicured and her hair styled and highlighted. She was never frivolous or high-maintenance —her family couldn't afford that—but she cared about how she looked. She has a great eye for stylish clothes, but she never cared if they came from a high-end department store or Goodwill. But after her kidnapping, she'd returned home broken and insecure, a mere shell of the vibrant, daring best friend I'd grown up with.

In spite of the heaviness that I carry in my heart over Brynne's death, there's a part of my heart that rejoices to see Tessa blossoming again. I never knew my heart could be so conflicted.

"Yeah, I'm doing okay," I say. "I'm going to miss her. She was a very dear friend, but . . . I'm doing okay."

Tessa's expression carries a hint of sadness as she leans her head against the couch and looks at me. "I'm sorry, Alli. I didn't know her as well as you did, and I know she was, well, one of your best friends." She's being sincere, but I don't miss the note of wistfulness in her voice.

"Yes, she was one my best friends and someone who stepped into my life when I really needed someone."

Tessa's gaze lowers. "Because I was no longer there."

I don't answer right away, because she's right. Tessa wasn't there. She was somewhere else, searching for herself and sampling a world that took her places she probably wishes she'd never gone. I don't say this to her, though, because we've already crossed that bridge and burned it behind us.

"You came back though."

She lifts her eyes to mine, and we both smile.

"Well, someone had to keep an eye on you," she says.

"Oh, is that right?" I laugh. "You thought I couldn't

make it on my own? Is that it? That I needed the Great Tessa Williams to keep my life interesting and provide me with entertainment?"

"Nah," she says softly. "I'm through with entertaining people. But you can't deny that I've always kept your life interesting."

I catch the meaning behind her words about entertaining people. I know she has some regrets about going along with the in-crowd and caving in to peer pressure, and I want to tell her that she's not the only one with regrets, but I don't want to lose the thread of playful bantering that we've started, so I let it go.

"Oh, you sure have," I say. "Remember when we were in fourth grade, and you got this wild idea for us to camp out in your backyard, and your mom let us set up a tent?"

Tessa sits up and scoots closer. "Of course. *And?* It was a lot of fun. You're welcome."

I push aside a couch pillow and move in closer too. "Hmm, did you forget about the part when you somehow convinced me that you knew how to start a campfire and sent me off to gather twigs while you snuck in the house for a lighter?"

Tessa's face is a mask of incredulousness. "Uh, yeah, I knew exactly what I was doing, Alli. Which one of us had been a Girl Scout, huh?"

I snort. "Brownie. You were never a Girl Scout."

"Close enough," she huffs.

"And if you were so knowledgeable about starting a

fire," I continue, "why did you dump your dad's office trash over my twigs and smoke us out?"

Tessa picks up the end of one of her braids and points it at me. "The fire just hadn't caught on yet. It would have if my mom hadn't come traipsing out when she saw the smoke and dragged the hose over. I had everything under control."

I stare at her, my eyebrows raised. "Uh huh. That's what lots of people say moments before everything goes up in flames."

"Not even close, and you know it," Tessa rolls her eyes. "Alli Mancini, has there ever been a dull moment with me? Admit it. I'm the best thing that's ever happened to you!"

I reach over and tug on one of her braids. "Don't be so stuck on yourself."

We both break out laughing, and she knows she's got me. It's absolutely true; Tessa's one of the best things that's ever happened to me.

Suddenly, her face grows serious. "I'm glad you're doing better, Alli. I know this has been hard for you. You're one of the strongest girls I know."

I nod but don't say anything. Instead, I wait to see where Tessa is going next because I can see her hesitation in the way her eyes go soft and how she bites down on her bottom lip.

"Is there anything else going on?" she asks. "I mean, do you have anything else on your mind?"

I run through the recent history catalog in my brain,

but nothing stands out. "Uh, no . . . Like, college? My roommate, Harper? I'm lost."

She blinks and waits patiently for whatever reality she assumes will come to me.

It doesn't.

Rolling my hands toward her, I give her a puzzled look. "Help me out here, Tessa."

Her sigh is loud enough to fill the room. "Anthony. Remember him?"

I throw myself back against the couch. "Really, Tessa? We're fine. There's nothing concerning going on."

"That's exactly it! There's *nothing* going on, as in the *something* you guys had going has fizzled out to *nothing*," she says.

"What do you mean? What gave you that idea?" I feel the heat rising in my chest, and my defenses are suddenly in high alert. Then, I remember that for all she knows from all my whining over the phone with her, Anthony has been ignoring me, and our relationship is a big question mark. She doesn't know about the recent conversation I've had with him—that we really are fine.

She shrugs. "Okay, I might be making too much of this."

"Not *might,* more like *probably*," I say. "In fact, we—"

"You guys are supposed to be dating, right?" she interrupts. "So why did you guys not say one word to each other at Brynne's service? Wouldn't that experience have driven you guys to be inseparable that day instead of a million miles apart from each other?"

"Tessa, you *are* making too much of this. Anthony and I talked on the phone for an hour that morning, and I warned him that I would need some space for a few days. He agreed to give me all the space I needed and said he would call me the next day—which he did. I haven't had a chance to update you—"

"Okay, hang on . . . I'm sorry," she interrupts again, hands held up in surrender. "You're right. I was going off appearances and thought you guys had cooled things off and weren't talking. I guess I shouldn't have assumed things weren't going well with you guys. I should have talked to you first, or—and this is hard to do because you're my best friend—I should have minded my own business. Forgive me?"

"Yes, I forgive you. But, well . . . you're right, in a way. Things *have* been different between us, but—as I've been trying to say, but you keep interrupting—we talked about it. He's had a lot going on, and, well, he didn't realize that I was in the dark about it all. I still don't know what the future holds for us, but we're just taking it a day at a time." I shrug. "It's hard though. *Really* hard sometimes."

Tessa reaches for my hand and gives it a squeeze. "Aw, I'm sorry, girl. I'm glad you two talked. Do you think this whole long-distance relationship might not work for you guys? You can really care about someone but not be able to have a meaningful relationship because you hardly get to see each other."

That isn't what I want to hear. Of course, I've been thinking the exact same thing, but I don't want it to be true. "I don't know, Tessa. I think—I *hope* Anthony and I are stronger than that."

"Even the best couples don't survive it sometimes, Alli. But"—she hurries to add, probably sensing that she's making things worse— "it's not impossible. My Aunt Carissa and her husband dated their last two years of college, and they both went to colleges that were five hundred miles apart from each other. That was before the days of FaceTime, too."

I give her a brave smile. "Thanks, Tessa. That gives me hope."

"Have you talked about, you know, what Anthony thinks about all this? Does he still see you in his future?"

I shake my head. "We haven't really talked about it. I guess I don't know how. I mean, what do I say? Am I supposed to come right out and ask, 'So Anthony, are you tired of doing this? Do you wish you had a girlfriend who lived closer and who you could actually spend time with?'" I throw my hands in the air. "I'm just no good at this, Tessa. Do you know how long it took for me to figure out this whole dating thing as it is? We were talking and flirting for weeks before I finally came right out and asked him if he considered me his girlfriend." I frown slightly. "Actually, now that I think of it, I believe my exact words were 'Are we a *thing* now?'"

Tessa cups her hands under her chin and gives me her best puppy-eyes. "Oh, how romantic. How did he answer?"

"He said he thought that was pretty obvious already." I sigh. "See how clueless I am about this kind of stuff?"

I glance at Tessa, expecting to see her nodding in agreement, but her face is a mask of compassion. "You're doing just fine. But you might have to consider that he might be assuming—again—that what's going on between you two is *obvious* when it really isn't obvious for you at all. That's why you have to talk to him, Alli. Communication is super important."

I find myself nodding in agreement. "You know, Tessa, you would make a great marriage counselor."

She giggles. "Nah, I'd make more money as a veterinarian."

Chapter Thirty-Four

I'M SHOPPING AT TARGET, LOOKING FOR A DECORATIVE basket to keep my books in when Tessa calls. I smile when I recognize the ring tone.

"What's up?" I answer.

"Guess what?" Tessa sounds eager, so whatever she has to say must be exciting.

I'm already smiling. "I give. What?"

"Are you sitting down?" she asks.

"Do I have to be? Hang on." I walk to the end of the aisle I'm in and look toward the lawn and garden area. Making my way over to a patio chair, I sit down. "Okay. I'm sitting. Oh, wait! You got accepted into a college?"

I stand.

Tessa groans. "More on that later. This is better. Shanice is coming to church with me on Sunday!"

This time, I really do need to sit. "No way! You're joking! How did that happen?"

"Well," she says, "you know that we've gone shopping a few times and that she's come over to hang out once or twice, right?"

"Yeah. And how you also told me that she's never invited you to *her* house. But that's beside the point. Go on."

"Focus, Alli. So, she comes over the other night, and we're just chilling on the couch. Anyhow, my mom asks her if she wants to stay for dinner, and she does."

My mind wanders to all the meals I've been part of at the Williams' house, and I can't help but feel a little jealous. Not that Shanice is a threat between me and Tessa, but, well, I'm human.

"Never thought I'd see the day that Shanice would—" I start to say something sarcastic, but she doesn't let me finish.

"—Would you just listen?!" Tessa groans. "Well," she continues. "So, my mom brings up Friends Sunday—"

"Oh, I miss Friends Sundays!" I say.

Tessa huffs with impatience. "*Sooo* Shanice is like, 'What's Friends Sunday?' and I tell her that it's when we're supposed to bring a friend and that there's a potluck afterward and all that. She goes, 'Oh, that sounds cool.' Then, of course, my mom gives me this look across the table that—well, you know my mom—screams that Shanice's comment is my cue to, you know, invite her. Ugh, it's the last thing I wanted to do."

I nod and say, "Oh, yeah. Talk about feeling cornered."

"Yeah, exactly." She sighs. "Anyhow, what else could I do? I asked Shanice if she wanted to come, thinking, of course, that the high-and-mighty Shanice wouldn't be caught dead in a church, especially not your—*our*—church. She tortured you about being a Christian, especially about being Apostolic and how different you look from everyone else—how different I've started looking too, how I dress and all that. Don't get too excited, Alli, I'm still a work in progress." She takes a breath. "So, anyway, imagine how shocked I was when she said yes! Inside, I'm like, *You have to be kidding me.* And just like that, I'm bringing a sort-of friend to Friends Sunday! Can you believe it?"

I'm not lying one bit when I tell Tessa that I absolutely don't believe it, but it's really happening, whether I believe it or not. We chat for a few more minutes before I tell her I need to finish my shopping, but I make her promise to call me the minute she gets home on Sunday and update me on how things went.

Wonder of wonders. Shanice Bradshaw, going to church.

God surely does work in mysterious ways.

Chapter Thirty-Five

Professor Anzler finishes his lecture and turns his attention to a book on his desk. Lifting the novel, *House of Mirth* by Edith Wharton, he displays the cover for the class to see.

"I assume you've all gotten your copy of this book," he says, flashing a smile that I'm sure sends half the girls in class into a swoon. "Read the first three chapters and be ready to discuss them next Tuesday in class. Sorry, ladies, this one's going to be a hard read for you when it comes to Lily's character." He tosses the book back on his desk and looks at his watch. "Well, there's only five minutes left of class, so feel free to pack up."

I've already packed up my notebook and pencil, and I fish out my cell phone to browse through. I could chat with some of my classmates instead, but I'm not feeling it. To be honest, I've become a bit of a hermit in this class since the internship shipwreck, and I've been avoiding Professor Anzler ever since. I started sitting closer to the door so that when it's time to leave, I'm the first one out of class. Anzler hasn't mentioned the internship since our last chat, and neither have I.

I prefer to keep it that way.

I'm scrolling social media on my phone when I feel a presence stop in front of me. Of course it's Professor Anzler. I thought about him, and he appeared: Murphy's Law.

"How's it going, Alli?" His smile doesn't reach his eyes.

The old Alli would have sat up straighter and given my best impression of a doting student with no complaints. But I'm not feeling that either. "Good." I give a brief, tight-lipped smile and let it fade just a quickly. I know I'm being unfair, but I just can't muster a positive attitude.

"Wonderful. Well . . ." I sense the hesitancy in his voice before he continues, "have a great rest of your day," he says and turns to walk away.

It's time to go, and everyone makes for the door. I stand and shoulder my backpack.

But I can't ignore the piercing stab in my heart. I stare at his retreating back, pushing aside my bitterness and rallying up a dose of compassion instead.

Time to move on and grow up, Alli.

"Professor Anzler?" I call out to him. He turns and

meets my eyes. There's a knowing there. I decide to leave it at that.

"Have a great rest of your day too."

Chapter Thirty-Six

I FEEL AN ARM GO AROUND ME AND PULL ME IN FOR A HUG as I stand at the altar after church, talking to God. I look up at Sister Reece, my youth pastor's wife, and see tears in her eyes. I know she notices mine too.

"How are you doing, kiddo?" she asks and gives me a squeeze.

I slip an arm around her too. "Doing good, Sister Reece. I know you've been praying for me. I feel it."

She smiles and nods. "Always, Alli. You're in my prayers daily. I know that you've been through a lot this year and that you have a lot of decisions to make about your future. No matter what happens, I'm here for you."

I reach my other arm around and give her a full hug. "Thanks. I appreciate you so much."

I'd gone to Sister Reece a few weeks ago and asked if

we could meet. I needed to talk to someone who would understand and offer a neutral opinion.

She agreed, and we met at her house, talking while her kids played in the next room.

I unloaded everything on her, from my relationship with Anthony and what his new ministry might mean for us, to struggling with my identity as a Christian and a young woman. She listened, never interrupting except to check on the kids and make us coffee. She spoke words of wisdom and encouragement, and she prayed with me. "Only you and God know your true heart, Alli. Seek to align your heart with God's, and it will all come together. I promise," she told me.

I felt like a mountain had lifted off my shoulders that afternoon.

As I was leaving, she reminded me of God's word: "'Favor is deceitful,' Alli, 'and beauty is vain,'" she said. "'But a woman that fears the Lord, she will be praised. Give her of the fruit of her hands and let her own words praise her in the gates.'"

"Proverbs 31, right?" I said.

"Correct." She looked pleased that I recognized the verses. "You are worth waiting for, Alli. College isn't forever. If Anthony is the one God has for you, he'll be patient. Your true beauty is what you have inside, and I bet Anthony sees that for himself. If he's the godly man you've described to me, then he'll want a woman who fears the

Lord and is willing to work beside him in whatever ministry God calls him—and you—to."

"But what if it's me who doesn't want to wait?" I'd asked.

The look she gave me pierced straight to my heart. I knew what she was going to say before she spoke the words: "Then I think you and God have some things to work out."

Chapter Thirty-Seven

It's been a while since I've had a talk with Nonna Mancini.

Not a face-to-face one, because she's with Jesus now, but one of those talks where I imagine she's sitting across from me in her porch chair, sipping coffee from one of her favorite mugs, and allowing me to pour my problems out to her while she pours her love back on me.

I was due for one of those talks today. It couldn't be just anywhere though. I'd always felt closer to Nonna when we were outside in nature. There was usually some birdsong and the smell of flowers to set the mood for sharing and just being together.

The closest I can come to that experience is my favorite bench behind the college theater building, the large tree draping over me with its veil of protection. There's plenty of boisterous birds chirping and cackling to each other from the overhead branches. I even stopped by the campus coffee shop and picked up a hot latte to sip on. The only thing missing—and I feel its loss deeply—is Nonna's presence.

But I'll have to wait for that.

And for Brynne.

All the waiting and wondering.

It's hard growing up, Nonna. I'm just getting started, but I'm feeling a little overwhelmed with it all already. But it's getting better. I have a lot of people who love me and keep me going. I mean, what would I do without Mom reminding me to wash my sheets every week? Was she like that growing up? I laugh out loud on that one, then quickly glance around to make sure no one's spying on me.

There's no one in sight.

Then there's Dad, who's the only Mancini keeping the rest of us grounded. And Avery, who depends on me to forge the way for her as she follows behind me. You already know what Tessa means to me. Everyone should have a best friend like Tessa. She needs me too, Nonna, and it's nice to be needed. I wish you could have met Anthony. You would've approved. I'll keep you updated on what happens with us. We're still figuring things out. I've made some new friends too, but, well, I'm still figuring those relationships out too.

And . . . Brynne. I guess you've already met Brynne. Isn't she awesome? I think so too. I miss her.

And I miss you, Nonna.

But I want you to know that I'm going to be okay—even with all this adulting stuff.

I hold my coffee cup up in a cheer to the sky, then bring

the cup to my lips. *This one's for you, Nonna. I'm not sure there's coffee in Heaven or if you even care, but it's what we did together, right? Drink coffee? So, I'll just imagine you're here with me, if that's alright.*

I close my eyes and try to imagine her face, her smile, her wrinkled hand reaching out to grab mine. I take in the birds, the breeze on my face, the smell of the honeysuckle bushes against the theater wall behind me.

Nonna would have loved those honeysuckle bushes.

I sigh and suck in the tears that threaten to come. I didn't come here to cry. I don't want Nonna to think I have to cry every time I talk to her.

I'm a maturing woman now, or at least I'm trying to be.

Chapter Thirty-Eight

TESSA CALLED ME AFTER SHANICE'S VISIT TO CHURCH ON Friends Sunday and told me that Shanice had looked like she wanted to flee out the back doors the whole service but seemed to relax a bit during the potluck afterward.

I laughed. "Baby steps. She's heard some crazy rumors about our church, so I'm surprised she was even brave enough to go. Do you think she'll want to go back?"

"Well," Tessa said. "I asked her what she thought of the service, and she just shrugged and said it was different. I have no idea what she meant by *different*, but, hey, she still wants to hang out, so that's saying something. My mom says I should ask her to a youth game night and see if she feels more comfortable there. Who knows, maybe I will."

I think about that conversation with Tessa now. Tessa's barely learning how to be a Christian herself and is still deciding if she's all in, but, like I said, baby steps. She'll also be learning about Anthony's new position as her youth pastor soon—I had kept Anthony's news a secret, as he'd asked. I know it's going to be a good thing . . . for everyone.

I'm unexpectedly filled with sadness and longing. If and when Shanice comes back to church, I want to be there. She'd been my nemesis and had hated anything to do with church, but now the tides are changing, and I'm missing it all.

Sister Reece's words come back to me. "Only you and God know your true heart, Alli."

Well, God, at least one of us does. I'd love for you to help me know my heart in all of this.

Chapter Thirty-Nine

THE LIBRARY GUY, WHO I NOW KNOW IS NAMED QUINCY, cocks his head and smiles down at me.

"So, you're a Christian, a gifted writer, and a bookworm college girl. Am I missing anything from your list of accolades, or are there any other amazing titles I should grace you with?"

I laugh.

"Well, I'm still working on the gifted writer title." I smile. "But I won't deny I'm a Christian, and that's something I'll be working on the rest of my life."

"Ms. Aspiring Gifted Writer Christian-In-The-Works." Quincy taps a finger against his temple. "I'll work on remembering that, Allisandra."

An unexpected rush of gratitude and peace washes over me as a confident assurance of who I am as a woman of

God awakens within me. I think I might feel a little bolder and courageous too.

"You know, only my nonna called me Allisandra—well, and my mom when she's irritated with me. But you can just call me Alli."

Quincy nods, one black curl bouncing against his forehead. His green eyes regard me thoughtfully. "Alright, *Alli*. Since we're revealing nicknames to each other now, mine's Quincy." His expression is so serious that I'm not sure if he's teasing or not.

"Um," I say hesitantly. "That's not a nickname if that's your actual name . . . Quincy."

He raises his eyebrows, leans closer, and whispers in a conspiratorial voice, "I don't share this with just anyone, but . . ." He stops and looks to see if anyone else is around, adding to the suspense. "It's *how* you say it; emphasis on the *cy* at the end. You know, Quin*cy*. Got it?"

I bust out laughing. "You are such a goon," I lower my voice to add, "Quin*cy*."

He grins and gives me a wink. "Now you've got it."

It's my turn to look to see who's around. I don't know why I get so nervous and self-conscious about this. *Well, here goes.*

"Quincy," I start, leaving off the emphasis this time, "would you be interested in coming to church with me sometime? Like, this Sunday maybe?"

Quincy's expression turns serious, and he takes a step back. "I've got a girlfriend, Alli."

I shake my head and roll my eyes. "I'm not asking you on a date, silly. I've got a boyfriend anyway. It's church. You don't even have to sit next to me. In fact," I add, the thought just coming to me, "why don't you bring your girlfriend too? What's her name, by the way?"

Running a finger across his lips, I can tell he's at least considering my invitation. "I'll think about it. I'll see what Margo's—that's her name, my girlfriend—got going on this weekend." He reaches under the counter, pulls out a library business card, and turns it over. Then, he reaches for a pen out of a cup next to him. He slides both across the counter to me.

"Jot down the address and the time it starts. It's not, like, one of those sunrise services or anything is it?"

I smile as I write. "No, that's usually an Easter thing, and I don't know that we even have sunrise services at my church." I finish writing and pass the card and pen over to Quincy. "Here you go. I wrote my phone number down too," I say, pointing down at the card. "I hope you guys come. I'll be looking for you."

He shrugs and tucks the card into his back pocket. "Don't count on us just yet. Margo's a little funny about religion and all that stuff. I'm cool with it though. My sister and I used to get picked up by the bus ministry for the Baptist church, which I'm sure my mom used as a babysitting service, so I've been around it and know some of the Bible stories, you know?"

Well, Lord, a few Bible stories is a good place to start.

"Well, you tell Margo that no one will shove a church tract down her throat or call down fire and brimstone on her. Everyone's really friendly. Plus, I'll be there! How bad can it be?"

Quincy laughs and pats his back pocket. "Okay. I'll text you if Margo's up for it. Go work on perfecting that writing. Maybe we'll carry one of your books here at the library someday."

Chapter Forty

"I'm coming home."

As soon as the words leave my mouth, I start to cry. They aren't tears of regret or a confession of failure on my part. These are tears of relief. Heartfelt, deep relief. It took me a while to come to terms with them and admit them to another human, but I'm ready now.

Tessa is silent, which makes me super nervous because I fully expected her to either start screaming with joy or come right out and accuse me of lying. The fact that she isn't saying *anything* throws me off.

"Tessa?"

"I heard," is her only response.

Sniffling, I mumble, "This is the part where you're supposed to start crying with me and say something like, 'Oh, Alli, this is the best news ever!' You know, something more than 'I heard.'"

"Why?"

"Why what?" I huff. "What's so hard about this? I'm coming home, Tessa. Like . . . home to Tucson. Home to stay. As in withdrawing from college. *Home.*"

"Why are you doing this?" Her voice cracks on the last word, and I think, *Finally, my words are hitting home.* "Because this was all a mistake." I instantly regret the way the words sound and try again. "No, not a mistake. Coming to California has been a learning and growing experience for me. I needed this time to be on my own and think about what I really wanted in life instead of just running away from my problems and believing they would all go away by moving here—or by moving anywhere."

"What's really going on, Alli? What happened?" The emotion behind her words hits me all at once, and I realize that she hasn't had the time to process this decision the way that I have and that, naturally, she'd think something awful has happened to prompt my sudden decision to walk away from college and California. But it's not a sudden decision. I've been wrestling with it, praying over it, and writing and rewriting pros and cons lists over it for weeks now.

My parents had been just as shocked as Tessa is right now. And I haven't even called Anthony yet, so that should be another interesting and exciting conversation. So, I guess I should have expected this. Mom, Dad, Tessa . . . this is their first time hearing about my life-changing decision, while I've been hearing all about it in my head for weeks from the moment I woke up in the morning until I crawled into bed at night, with many middle-of-the-night over-thinking sessions thrown in as well.

"Tessa, hear me out. Nothing's wrong. I promise. In fact, everything feels better than it has in a long time. I wanted to come to California to start over, go to college, and figure some things out. You already know all this. You remember how I struggled with this decision and my reasons for coming here. But you also know that the things I claimed I wanted from coming here weren't the real reasons." I take a breath. "The point is, I know that now, and, well, that's why I've decided to come home."

"Was it because of me?" Tessa asks. "I mean, I know you wanted to get as far away as possible from Chad, Shanice, and that whole crowd, and I know you wanted to figure out what your future held in a new place, but was one of your reasons because of what I'd put you through?"

How did this conversation become so complicated all of a sudden?

"What? No. What are you talking about? Of course, I wasn't running away from you, Tessa. Why would you think that? I wasn't even running away from the crowd at West Morrison High. In fact, even though I'd started to believe that it might be possible, hiding from God wasn't even an option. I think the one I was running from turned out to be myself." I shake my head in frustration. "I know this doesn't make any sense, but—"

"It does," Tessa interrupts. "I think I know exactly what you mean. In fact, I can't tell you how many times I cried myself to sleep at night, Alli, wishing I could run away from myself. There were times I felt like I could make peace with what happened to me, with people who used me for their own gain, and with people I thought were my friends but who turned me out the minute trouble showed up. And, no, I'm not talking about you; that was just a rough patch in our friendship.

To those others, I could slam the door to my room in their faces at night and deal with them and the memories later. But I couldn't do that with Tessa Williams. No matter how I tried, she shadowed me everywhere I went, haunting my dreams. I couldn't run away from what she'd done or make any kind of peace with decisions that she made. I still can't, and I honestly believe I never completely will.

So, I may not know what it's like to be targeted because of my faith or to be on the receiving end of a cruel prank like you were, but I know what it feels like to wish you could be anywhere in the world but in the same room with your-self. But believe it or not, I've been talking to God lately about it all. I'm getting better at doing that."

"Oh, Tessa . . ." I feel like a deflated balloon. I knew that Tessa had gone through a deep depression, but I hated that she still carried so many of those scars even now.

"I'm sorry, Alli. You called to share what you thought would be great news—and trust me, I'm doing somersaults of joy inside—but I want to make sure it's what you really want to do. That you aren't . . . Okay, don't get mad at me for saying this. Just promise me you aren't running away from something again."

"I'm not, Tessa. I'm being totally transparent here. I know what I need to do. I'm coming home. End of story. And if you don't start acting a little more excited about this, I'm going to hang up and never speak to you again."

I'm so relieved when she busts out laughing. "You wouldn't last a day. But you've convinced me. Ready, set, go! *Yes!* I can't believe you're coming home, Alli!" Tessa screams so loud that I jerk the phone away and hold it at arm's length.

When she's done, I press it back to my ear. "Well, it's about time you acted like a best friend and got on board. I was beginning to wonder if someone had replaced the real Tessa with a low-rated decoy."

"That's impossible," Tessa says. "A cheap substitute could never replace the real me. I'm one of a kind."

"Yes," I say with enthusiasm. "I agree. No one could ever replace you, Tessa Williams. Not for me anyway."

"So . . . when?" she asks.

"When what?"

"When are you coming home?"

"Oh, yes, home. Well, summer finals are over, and Harper is heading home next week. I'm taking her to see another play the college drama department is putting on to smooth things over. She's freaking out about getting a new roommate in the fall. But after that . . . Well, is next week too early?"

Tessa lets out a shriek that would wake the dead.

I join her. In fact, I might even be louder.

"Come home, Alli!" she yells. "We'll both take classes here, and I'll help you study and everything!"

"Am I really that helpless without you, Tessa?" I giggle "I *have* made it through my first year of college on my own you know."

"Fine. Noted. You've done a pretty good job, Alli Mancini. But we need you here."

"I've been hoping to hear those words, Tessa, and I need you all too. That's why I'm coming home—where I belong."

Did You Enjoy This Book?

~

If you enjoyed this book, I hope you will consider leaving a review on Amazon. Reviews are so important to an author. Even just a line or two can make a huge impact!

WWW.AMAZON.COM/DP/B0CPWM2JNF

SUBSCRIBE TO REGINA'S NEWSLETTER:

WWW.RLFELTY.COM/NEWSLETTER

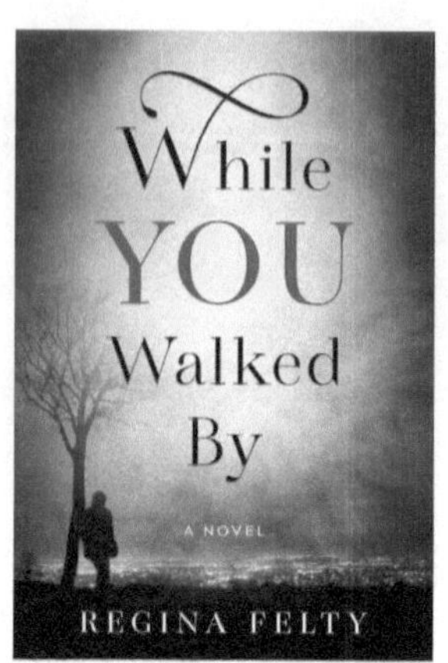
While
YOU
Walked
By
A NOVEL
REGINA FELTY